Alexander glanced around the room, understanding where he was. Not in Aargau but in Greece, on this island with Josephine, who'd rescued him.

He looked over and there she was, still sleeping in the bed. Her bed. Her cottage. Her island, not his.

Her long honey hair spilled across her bare shoulder. She was stunning even in her sleep. His very own mermaid.

She'd saved him. He would have died—drowned— if not for her, and when he was still weak, she'd taken care of him. And then last night she'd told him she loved him, and he hadn't answered her with words, but he'd shown her how much her faith in him mattered to him by making love to her for hours, worshipping her body since something inside him kept him from giving her his heart.

He'd thought that maybe he couldn't give himself to her fully because he didn't know who he was. But now he knew why he couldn't love her. Because she wasn't his, and he wasn't free.

He was Prince Alexander Julius Alberici of Aargau, and he was betrothed to another.

New York Times and *USA TODAY* bestselling author **Jane Porter** has written forty romances and eleven women's fiction novels since her first sale to Harlequin in 2000. A five-time RITA® Award finalist, Jane is known for her passionate, emotional and sensual novels, and loves nothing more than alpha heroes, exotic locations and happily-ever-afters. Today Jane lives in sunny San Clemente, California, with her surfer husband and three sons. Visit janeporter.com.

Jane Porter

THE PRINCE'S SCANDALOUS WEDDING VOW

Recycling programs
for this product may
not exist in your area.

ISBN-13: 978-1-335-53808-6

The Prince's Scandalous Wedding Vow

First North American publication 2019

Copyright © 2019 by Jane Porter

Printed in U.S.A.

THE PRINCE'S
SCANDALOUS
WEDDING VOW

For Lee Hyat.

Thank you for being my first reader, my friend and my cheerleader.

This one is for you!

PROLOGUE

PRINCE ALEXANDER JULIUS ALBERICI had known change was coming. His June 27 wedding to Princess Danielle would require a return to his Mediterranean island kingdom, Aargau, for prewedding festivities. After the ceremony and reception, a two-week honeymoon had been planned, and then he'd finally be free to return to Paris with his bride, where he oversaw an international environmentalist group focused on improving sustainability in fragile ecosystems.

His work was his passion, and Danielle had expressed support for his work—a positive in an arranged marriage. She'd also agreed at the time of their betrothal to live wherever he chose, understanding that ultimately they'd end up in Aargau as soon as Alexander needed to step into his father's shoes and ascend the throne.

But that day—replacing his father—was supposed to have been years away, decades away, as his father was a strong, athletic man and a vigorous, powerful king. Or he had been, until his winter cold lingered into early spring, a nagging cough that wouldn't clear even with antibiotics. And then in mid-April came the diagnosis of lung cancer and now King Bruno Titus Alberici had been given months to live. *Months.*

It was unthinkable, unfathomable. Alexander had never been close to his father—King Bruno might be beloved by the people, but he was cold and unforgiving behind closed doors—yet Alexander couldn't imagine the world without his fierce, unapologetic father. Now his father was determined to manage his death, just as he'd managed his life—without emotion or weakness. To that end, there would be no changes in palace life or protocol. Alexander's late-June wedding would not be moved forward. Bruno's illness would not be made public. There would be no changes in wedding date or venue. There would be no acknowledgment of ill health. There would be nothing to alarm the people until an announcement had to be made, which in King Alberici's mind was notice of his death.

His mother, the queen, agreed with the plan because that was what she did—supported her husband. It had been her role from day one of their marriage, and she'd fulfilled her responsibilities. Now it was time for Alexander to fulfill his, which was to marry and have an heir so the monarchy would live on.

Alexander stirred restlessly, feeling trapped in his cabin, even though it was by far the largest on the ship. He pushed open the sliding door and stepped out onto the balcony, leaning on the railing to stare blindly out at the sea.

This trip, organized by his closest friends, had been a mistake. He couldn't relax. He felt guilty being on a pleasure cruise when his father was growing weaker at home, and yet both his parents had insisted he go, determined that he keep up appearances.

The trip was to have been a last hurrah before the wedding preparations began in earnest. Princes didn't do bachelor or stag parties, so instead, Prince Alexander Alberici's best friend, Gerard, had organized a week cruising the Aegean and Ionian Seas. Troubled by his father's swift decline, Alexander had left the details to his friends, knowing they were far more excited about this last adventure—concerned that it might indeed be their last adventure—but now wished he'd been part of the planning, at least when it came to approving the guest list.

The yacht itself was impressive. Large, new, and the very definition of luxurious, with two different pools, a hot tub, a sports court, a disco, and a movie theater. But the luxurious appointments couldn't make up for the fact that it was a boat, and they were all trapped together—not a problem if everyone was on good terms, but inexplicably Gerard had permitted Alexander's cousin,

Damian Anton Alberici, to bring his girlfriend, Claudia, along.

It wouldn't have been an issue if Claudia didn't also happen to be Alexander's ex-girlfriend, and their breakup six months earlier had been acrimonious at best. He'd been stunned and uncomfortable when he discovered Damian was now dating Claudia, but to bring her on this trip? Why make it awkward for everyone?

Alexander's jaw tightened, his gaze narrowed on the pale rocky island ahead, each island so like the last.

The tension on the yacht just made him eager to return home, which was saying something as home wasn't exactly pleasant, either. His mother was struggling to come to terms with his father's terminal diagnosis. Virtually overnight his father had wasted away, his strong frame increasingly frail. The palace staff, sworn to secrecy, were incredibly anxious, tiptoeing around, walking on eggshells. And yet no one discussed what was happening. But that was because they didn't talk in his family, not about personal things. There was no sharing of feelings and certainly no acknowledgment of emotions. There was only duty, and he understood that all too well.

The sooner the wedding took place, the better, and Princess Danielle Roulet would be a good match. She was lovely and well-bred, and fluent in numerous languages, which was essential in Aargau's next queen. She was also sophisticated and would be a stylish princess, something he knew his people would appreciate. It was not a love match, but it would be a successful marriage because they both understood their duties and responsibilities, and best of all, the wedding would give the people of Aargau something to celebrate, which was sorely needed when the crown would soon change hands.

Now, if he could only get off this yacht and get back to his family—who did need him, despite what his parents might say, or not say—because Alexander was finding nothing pleasurable in this last bachelor getaway.

CHAPTER ONE

JOSEPHINE JUST WANTED the yacht to leave.

Why was it still here? The Mediterranean was huge. Greece alone had hundreds of islands. Couldn't the yacht go somewhere else? The luxury pleasure boat had been anchored outside the cove of her tiny island, Khronos, for two days, and after forty-eight hours of endless partying, blaring music, and shrill laughter, she'd had enough.

The revelers had even come onto the island earlier in the day, their testosterone-fueled speedboat racing them to shore. Jo had hidden behind the cliffs and trees above, watching as the dozen hedonists descended on her beach.

The young women were stunning—tan, lithe, and beautiful in tiny, barely-there bikinis—and the men were lean, chiseled, and handsome. While the women splashed in the surf and then lounged on the beach, the men sprawled on chairs and towels in the sun, looking like indolent princes. They were there to party, too, and there was plenty of alcohol and other things that made Josephine wrinkle her nose in disgust. Only one of them didn't drink, or smoke, or make love on the beach. Sometimes he sat on his own, but other times, people surrounded him. He was clearly the center of the group, the one with the wealth, the sun around which all the others orbited.

She watched the revelers out of curiosity and with a sprinkling of disdain, telling herself not to judge, but the interlopers on her beach clearly enjoyed a pampered, decadent lifestyle, a lifestyle for those born of privilege, or those lucky enough to be invited into the elite circle. Her dad used to say she was critical of such people because she'd never be one of them, and maybe there was some truth in that. But she liked to use her brain, and she enjoyed her work assisting her father, who was one of the world's leading volcanologists, which was why they lived in the middle of the Aegean Sea, taking advantage of Greece's volcanic arc.

Her work included documenting her father's findings, and she'd proved indispensable to his research. He was the first to admit that he wouldn't have his enormous body of work without her assistance. But late in the day, she'd turn to her passion—drawing, sketching, painting. She had run low on paper and canvas again, but her father would be returning in ten days, and he always brought back fresh supplies for her.

This afternoon she carried her sketch pad with her to the rocks overlooking the sheltered beach cove, thinking she'd draw the scene below—well, not everyone, but the one who'd caught her attention. The one man she thought was by far the most fascinating. He appeared otherworldly with his thick dark hair and straight black brows over light-colored eyes—blue or gray she didn't know. But even from a distance the lines of his face appealed to the artist in her: his jaw was square, cheekbones high, his mouth full, firm, unsmiling.

Her charcoal pencil hovered over the page as she studied the face she'd drawn. His features were almost too perfect, his lower lip slightly fuller than his upper lip, and she just wished she was closer so she could see the color of his eyes.

Even more intriguing was the way he sat in his chair, broad shoulders level, chin up, body still, exuding power and control. Josephine glanced up from the sketch to compare her work to the real man, and yes, she'd captured the sinewy, muscular frame as well as the hard set of his jaw and chin, but his expression wasn't quite right. It was his expression that intrigued her and made her want to keep looking at him and trying to understand him. Was he bored, or unhappy? Why did he look as if he wanted to be anywhere but on that beach, with these people?

He was a mystery, and she enjoyed a good puzzle. It gave her mind something to focus on, but now he was rising, and everyone else was rising, gathering their things and heading to the boat.

Good, she told herself, closing her sketchbook, and yet she couldn't help feeling a stab of disappointment as the speedboat whisked her mystery man back to the massive yacht anchored outside her cove, because he was, without a doubt, the most interesting man she'd ever seen, and now he was gone.

Later that evening, Josephine was returning from doing her last check of the equipment in the cottage when she heard loud voices, as if in argument, from just outside the cove. She crossed to the beach, listening intently, but this time she heard nothing, just the sound of the yacht engine humming. Was the yacht finally leaving?

As usual, it was brightly lit and pulsing with music. On the top deck she could see couples lounging and drinking. There were others on a deck below and then others at the far end of the yacht, in the shadows.

The yacht was moving. She could see the moonlight reflecting off the white wake. She was sorry to see her mystery man leave, but glad the noise would be gone. The music was terrible. She was still standing there when she heard a muffled shout and then saw someone go overboard. It was at the back of the yacht, where people had been on a lower deck in the shadows.

She rushed closer to the water's edge, attention fixed on the point where the person had gone into the water, but no one resurfaced. Sick, panicked, Josephine worried that someone could be drowning. She couldn't just stand idle while someone died.

She yanked off her sundress and dived between the waves to swim out to where the yacht had been anchored for the past two and a half days. Diving beneath the surface of the water, she struggled to see in the gloom, but all was dark, so dark, and the reef dropped off dramatically not far from her, the coral giving way to deep water. Josephine swam with her hands in front of her, searching, reaching, lungs burning, bursting, and just when she was going to push back to the surface, she felt fabric, and then heat. A chest. Shoulders. Big, thick shoulders. A man.

She prayed for help as she circled his neck with her arm, hoping for divine strength because she needed superpowers in that moment, her own lungs seizing, desperate for air.

With a groan, she pulled up and he rose with her. Not quickly, but he was floating as she swam, his huge body heavy, but she'd never swum with such resolve. She'd grown up in the ocean. She'd spent her life swimming, deep, exploring caves and the reef, and even though spots danced before her eyes she told herself she could do this because she wasn't alone. She had faith that she was meant to be there when the body fell overboard, and she was meant to find him, and she was meant to save him.

And she did.

She surfaced and, gasping for air, towed him to shore. Once she'd dragged him out of the waves, she kept pulling, hoping she wasn't hurting him as she wrestled him onto the firm damp sand. Once she knew they were out of the surf, she rolled him onto his side, allowing water to drain from his mouth and nose, before settling him onto his back. It was only then she realized it was him.

The beautiful brooding man.

The one who'd barely seemed to tolerate the others.

The one who suffered no fools.

She'd never had to resuscitate anyone before, but her father had taught her years ago, and she remembered the basics, although guidelines kept changing every year or two. She pinched his nose closed and then breathed into his mouth with five strong breaths, followed by thirty chest compressions. She put her ear near his mouth and listened. Nothing. She heard nothing. She repeated the cycle with two strong breaths into his mouth and another thirty compressions. After each cycle, she listened and watched his chest, checking for signs of life.

She wouldn't give up. *Breathe, breathe, breathe*, she chanted in her head, repeating the cycle, praying as she did, asking for divine help, not at all prepared to lose him.

Breathe, breathe, breathe.
Live, live, live.

Just when she was sure her efforts were pointless, his chest lifted—not much, but it moved, and it was enough to give her hope. Determined, Jo breathed into his mouth, those two strong breaths, and this time she felt air exhale from his lips and saw a definite rise and fall of his chest. His breath was rough and raspy, but it was a breath. It wasn't her imagination. He was alive.

Her eyes stung with tears. Her hands began to shake as she shoved her long, wet hair behind her ears, overwhelmed and exhausted. The sheer enormity of it all hit her, and she sat back on her heels, shoulders sagging. She'd saved him. But now what? What was she to do with him?

Her adrenaline faded, and she began trembling in earnest, wiped out. She didn't know how she'd managed any of it. She was a good swimmer, a strong swimmer, but it was a miracle she'd been able to find him and pull him to the shore. He needed medical help, and she had no way to call for assistance. Her radio was broken. Her dad would be bringing a new one when he returned, but that wasn't for days. Ordinarily, she wouldn't mind being cut off—she'd gone weeks before without communication—but this was different.

Her brow creased as she glanced out toward the sea, the mouth of the cove empty, the moonlight reflecting brightly on the water, the only sign of the yacht a distant glow of yellow light on the horizon.

How did no one notice that he'd gone overboard? How could they go without him?

Gently, she stroked his hair back from his brow, only then noting the blood matting the thick hair at his temple. He was injured, and from the nasty gash on his forehead, he'd been injured before he'd fallen—or been pushed—overboard.

She'd heard raised voices. She'd heard a fight. It was what had drawn her attention—that and the hum of the yacht engine. From the mark on his brow it looked as if someone had struck him. Why?

He blinked, trying to focus. His head hurt. Pain radiated through him. He struggled to sit but the world tilted and swam around him. He blinked again, not understanding why everything was so blurry. It was almost as if he was underwater and yet, through the haze, he saw a woman leaning over him, her face above his, her expression worried.

He struggled to place her. How did he know her? Did he know her?

The effort to think was too much. He gave up trying to focus and closed his eyes, sinking back into oblivion.

Pain woke him again.

A heavy, brutal pounding in his head made him stir, his eyes slowly, carefully opening, trying to minimize the ache in his head.

It was day, either early or late he didn't know because the light was soft, diffused.

A woman was moving around the room. She wore a loose white dress, the gauzy fabric fluttering around her bare legs. She paused at the small square window, her brow creasing as she gazed out. Her hair was long and straight, falling almost to her waist.

For a moment he wondered if she was an angel. For a moment he wondered if he had died and gone to heaven. Not that he deserved to go to heaven. Strange thought, but true. He struggled to rise but immediately felt nauseous.

Biting back a curse, he slowly sank back against the pillow, realizing he wasn't dead—or at least, he wasn't in heaven. He couldn't be, not if he hurt this much.

His muffled groan must have reached the angel girl, as she turned in her white dress, the delicate fabric floating behind her as she moved toward him, so young, so beautiful he was certain she wasn't real.

Perhaps he was feverish. Perhaps he was hallucinating, because as she knelt next to him, the sun's rays seemed to narrow and cast a glow around her, highlighting her long golden-brown hair, her smooth brow, and the high, elegant cheekbones above her full lips.

Maybe hell was filled with angelic beauties.

* * *

He was finally coming to. Josephine moved forward, crouching at his side. "Hello," she said in English, before it struck her that it was unlikely English was his native language. Most of the conversation she'd heard on the beach had been French, while others had spoken Italian. "How are you?" she asked in French.

He blinked and struggled to focus, his eyes a brilliant blue, contrasting with his long, dense black lashes.

She tried Italian next. "How do you feel?"

His brow tightened. He grimaced, responding in Italian. *Tu chei sei?" Who are you?*

"Josephine," she answered, as he slowly reached up to touch his head, where a crust had formed on his cut. "Careful," she added in Italian. "You've been injured. It's finally stopped bleeding."

"What happened?"

"You went over the side of your yacht."

"A yacht?" he repeated in Italian.

"Yes. You were with friends."

"Dove sono?" he murmured, his voice a deep rasp. *Where am I?*

"Khronos. A small island off Anafi," she answered.

"I don't know it."

"Anafi is very small. No one knows Anafi, and Khronos is even smaller. It's privately held, a research site for the International Volcanic Research Foundation—" She broke off as she realized he wasn't listening, or at least, he wasn't processing what she was saying, his features tight with pain. "Do you hurt right now?"

He nodded once. "My head," he gritted.

She reached out to place a palm against his brow. He was cooler now, thank goodness. "You were running a fever last night, but I think it's gone now." She drew her hand back, studying him. "I'd like to see if you can manage some water, and if you can, then we'll try some soup—"

"I'm not hungry. I just want something for the pain."

"I have tablets that should help with the headache, but I think you should eat first. Otherwise I'm worried it'll upset your stomach."

He looked at her as if he didn't understand, or perhaps he didn't believe her, because his blue eyes were narrowing and his mouth firmed, emphasizing his strong jaw, now shadowed with a dark stubble.

He'd been striking from afar, but up close he was absolutely devastating, his black hair and brows such a contrast to his startlingly blue eyes. His features were mature and chiseled. Faint creases fanned from his eyes.

As his gaze met hers and held, her pulse jumped. "It's been almost a full day since I pulled you out of the sea—"

"How?" he interrupted.

"How?" she repeated.

"How did I get here?"

"Your boat. Your yacht—"

"I don't understand this yacht." The wrinkles in his forehead deepened. He struggled into a sitting position, wincing and cursing under his breath. His hand lifted to his temple, where the wound was beginning to bleed again. "When was I on one?"

"The past few days. Probably the past week or more." She sat back on her haunches, studying him. "Do you not remember?"

He shook his head.

"What do you remember?"

He thought for a moment, and then his broad, sun-bronzed shoulders shifted irritably, impatiently. "Nothing." His voice was hard, his diction crisp. Authority and tension crackled around him.

Her jaw dropped ever so slightly. "You don't remember who you are? Your name? Your age?"

"No. But I do know I need to find a bathroom. Can you show me the way?"

He had questions for her later, many questions, and Josephine fought to hide her anxiety over his complete loss of memory. She prepared them a simple dinner, talking to him as she plated the grilled vegetables and lemon-garlic chicken. "I think you must be Italian," she said, carrying the plates to the small rustic table in the center of the room. The table divided the room, creating the illusion of two spaces, the sitting area and then the kitchen. "It was the first language you responded to."

"I don't feel Italian." He grimaced. "Although I'm not sure what that even means. Can a person feel their nationality?"

"I don't know," she answered, sitting down across from him. "But I suppose if I woke up somewhere else I'd be puzzled by the different cultural norms."

"Tell me about the people I was with."

"They were all about your age. Although some of the girls seemed younger. They all looked… polished. Affluent." She hesitated. "Privileged."

He said nothing.

"Everyone seemed to be having a good time," she added. "Except for you."

He glanced at her swiftly, gaze narrowing.

"I don't know if you were bored, or troubled by something," she added, "but you tended to be off on your own more than the others. And they gave you your space, which made me think you were perhaps the leader."

"The leader?" he repeated mockingly. "The leader of what? A band of thieves? Pirates? Schoolboys on holiday?"

"You don't need to be rude," she said slowly, starting to rise, wanting to move away, but he reached out and caught her, his fingers circling her narrow wrist, holding her in place.

"Don't go."

She looked down to where his hand wrapped her wrist, his skin so very warm against hers. She suppressed a shudder, feeling undone. She was exhausted from watching over him, exhausted from worrying. It had been a long night and day, and now it was night again and she felt stretched to the breaking point. "I'm just trying to help you," she said quietly, tugging free.

He released her. "I'm sorry." His deep voice dropped. "Please sit. Stay."

His words were kind, but his tone was commanding. Clearly he was accustomed to being obeyed.

Her brow furrowed. She didn't want to create friction, and so she slowly sat back down and picked up her fork, but she felt too fatigued to actually eat.

Silence stretched. She could feel him watching her. His scrutiny wasn't making things easier, and she knew his eye color now. Blue, light, bright aquamarine blue. Blue like her sea. Reluctantly, she looked up, her stomach in knots. "I thought you were hungry," she said, aware that he hadn't yet taken a bite, either.

"I'm waiting for you."

"I've lost my appetite."

"The company you're keeping?"

She cracked a small smile. "The company's fine. I think I'm unusually tired tonight."

"I suspect you were up all night worrying about me."

It was true. She hadn't been sure he'd survive. There were complications for those who'd nearly drowned. "But you made it through, and here you are."

"Without a memory, or a name."

"I suppose we should call you something."

"Perhaps," he said, but it was clear from his tone that he didn't agree and wasn't enthusiastic about being called by a name that was probably not his.

"We could try names out, see if anything resonates."

He gave her a long, hard look that made her stomach do a funny little flip. "I'll say names and you tell me if anything feels right," she pressed on.

"Fine."

"Matthew. Mark. Luke. John."

"I'm fairly certain I'm not an apostle."

Her lips twitched. "You know your Bible stories, then."

"Yes, but I don't like this approach. I want my own name, or no name." He stabbed his fork into his dinner but made no attempt to eat. "Tell me about you," he said, turning the tables. "Why are you here on what appears to be a deserted island?"

"Well, it's not deserted—it's an island that serves a scientific purpose, housing one of the five research stations for the International Volcano Foundation. My father is a professor, a volcanologist. We were supposed to be here for a year but it's been almost eight."

"Where is he now?"

"Hawaii." She saw his expression and added, "He is a professor at the University of Hawaii. He juggles the teaching and the fieldwork. Right now he's back in Honolulu, lecturing, but he'll return end of the month, which is now just nine days away."

"And he has left you alone here?"

She hesitated. "Does it seem strange to you?"

"Yes."

Her shoulders shifted. "It's actually normal for me, and I don't mind. I like the solitude. I'm not much of a people person. And the quiet allows me a chance to do my own work, because when Papa is here, it's always about him."

"What about your mother?"

"She died just before I turned five."

"I'm sorry."

She shrugged again, uncomfortable with the sympathy. "I don't remember her."

"Would she approve of your lifestyle here?"

"She was a volcanologist like my father. They worked together for ten years, doing exactly what he's doing now, but in Hawaii, so yes, I think she'd approve. Perhaps her only disappointment would be that I haven't gone off to college or earned all the degrees that she did. I've been homeschooled my entire life, even with the university courses. My father says I'm more advanced than even his graduate students, but it's not the same. I've never had to be in the real world or compete with others for work. I just work."

"What is your field of study?"

"I'm a volcanologist, too, although personally I prefer the point where archaeology intersects with volcanology."

"Vesuvius?"

She nodded. "Exactly. I've been lucky to work with my father on the volcanology of the south-western sector of Vesuvius, where archaeological and historical data have allowed scientists to map the lava emitted in the last several thousand years. I'm fascinated by not just the lost civilizations, but the power of these volcanoes to reshape the land-scape and rewrite the history of man."

"It doesn't sound as if you've missed anything by being homeschooled."

She smiled faintly. "I haven't been properly so-cialized—my father said as much. I'm not com-fortable in cities and crowds. But fortunately, we don't have that problem here."

"Your mother was American, too?"

"French-Canadian, from Quebec. That's how I ended up Josephine." Her smile faded as she saw how his expression changed, his jaw tightening and lips compressing. "You *will* remember your name," she said quietly. "It's just going to be a matter of time."

"You spoke to me in French, didn't you?"

"I tried a number of languages. You responded in Italian, so I've stuck with Italian. *Est-ce que tu parles français?*"

"*Oui.*"

"And English?" she asked, switching languages again. "Do you understand me?"

He nodded. "I do."

"How fluent are you?" she asked, continuing in English, testing him. "Is it difficult to follow me?"

"No. It doesn't seem any different from Italian."

He had almost no accent, his English was easy, his diction relaxed, making him sound American, not British. She suspected he'd been educated at one point in the United States. "Would you mind speaking English then?"

"No."

"But should it give you a headache, or if it creates any stress—"

"No need to fuss over me. I'm fine."

She opened her mouth to protest but thought better of it. He was a man used to having the final word. So who was he? And why did he, even now, ooze power?

"Tell me again about the people I was with on the yacht," he said. "Tell me everything you know."

"I will after you eat something."

"I'm not hungry anymore."

"That's strange, because my memory seems to be fading, as well."

He gave her a hard look. "I'm not amused."

"Neither am I. You've been through a great deal, and we need to get you strong. And as I am your primary caregiver here—"

"I don't like being coddled."

"And I'm not known to coddle, so eat, and I'll tell you everything. Don't eat, and you can fret by yourself because I have things to do besides argue with you."

His eyes narrowed and his jaw hardened, making a small muscle in his jaw pop. For a long moment he just looked at her, clearly not happy with the situation, but then he reached for the plate of chicken and took a bite, and then another, and did a pretty impressive job of devouring the rest. He lifted his head at one point and met her gaze. "This is good, by the way. Very good."

"Thank you."

"You made this?"

"Yes."

"Here?"

"Yes."

"How?"

"I have a freezer, and I use the kiln outside for roasting the potatoes and baking. The rest I prepare on the stove."

"A kiln?"

"It makes excellent flatbreads, and pizzas, too. I learned how to cook in a kiln when we lived in Peru. That was before here. I loved Peru. My father loved the stratovolcano." She smiled faintly, remembering his excitement and obsession as Sabancaya roared to life, spewing ash and rumbling the mountain. If it weren't for the village women, Josephine would have been forgotten. Instead they took her and her father in and helped teach Josephine to cook, and as a thank-you, Josephine would look after the children, giving the hardworking mothers a break.

"Where else have you lived?"

"Washington State, Hawaii, Peru, and Italy, but that was brief, before here. We've been here the longest."

"Was every place this isolated?"

"No, this is definitely the most remote, but I'm truly happy here."

"Is that why you just watched us on the beach and didn't come introduce yourself?"

She laughed as she reached for his plate. "I think

we come from different worlds. I am quite sure I'd be an oddity in your world."

His brow creased. "You think so?"

"Absolutely. I wouldn't know how to drape myself over and around handsome men." Her lips twitched. "I can't for the life of me just lie on a beach. I need to be active, and instead of sunbathing I'd be catching fish, and examining the water table, and trying to figure out the volcanic history of the exposed rocks—" she broke off. "Not your kind of girl at all."

"What is my kind?"

"The kind that looks like a swimsuit model. The kind that doesn't lift anything, not even her own swim bag. The kind that pouts when you don't feel like talking."

"Interesting," he drawled, blue eyes glinting. "How so?"

"You didn't like my friends. You never said that earlier. This is new information."

"I shouldn't have said anything. It's not factual and not important—"

"But revealing about you."

"Exactly. There is no reason to share my feelings on anything. I should be focused on assisting you. Who I am and what I feel isn't relevant in any way."

"You're allowed to have opinions."

"I'll voice them if they'll be helpful. Me judging your female friends isn't helpful. It's just me being petty and unkind and unnecessary."

"Why do I feel like you are a rare breed?"

"Because I am strange. I don't fit in. I never have."

"Sounds a bit defeatist, don't you think?"

"I would agree with you if I were here licking my wounds. But I'm here by choice, because I'm happy here. I sleep well here. I can breathe here. I don't feel odd or different, and on Khronos I don't second-guess myself, and that's a good thing."

"You're saying society makes you uncomfortable."

"Absolutely." She carried his plate and fork to the small sink in her very small kitchen and felt his gaze bore into her back as she filled the small plastic dish tub with water to let them soak. "But I've been raised outside society so it's to be expected."

"Have you ever lived in a city?"

"Honolulu."

"Is that a proper city?"

She turned and shot him a disapproving look. "Yes. Honolulu has some beautiful architecture and it has a fascinating history. Hawaii isn't just beaches and surfing." She didn't tell him, though, that she didn't enjoy going back to Oahu anymore because it was too urban for her now. There were far too many cars and people and it had been overwhelming, which was why she'd elected to remain behind on Khronos while her father went to teach.

She turned away from the sink, wiped her hands dry on a dish towel and carried the water carafe to the table. "There were maybe twelve of you that came onto the beach," she said, taking her seat again. "Seven men, including you, and five women. The yacht was huge. One of the biggest, most luxurious yachts I've ever seen. Your group would come onto the beach during the day and everyone would swim and sunbathe, eat and drink." She shot him a long look. "There was lots of drinking. Everyone seemed to be having a good time."

"And the night I went overboard?"

"There was music playing—as always—and a party. As always. Your friends were on the top two decks—the top deck you all used as a disco, so the music and dancing were there, but there were others on the second deck, and I wasn't sure if they were in a hot tub or a pool, but people there were just hanging out, talking and laughing. But what got my attention on that last night was the arguing at the back of the yacht. I heard voices, or thought I heard voices, and things sounded like they were getting a little heated. It was what caught my attention and what drew me to the edge of the water."

"*I* was arguing?" he asked quietly.

She hesitated, frowning. "Yes. No. I don't actually know that it was you. I just heard arguing, and then there was a shout and a splash. I couldn't see that well and for a second wondered if someone had maybe jumped overboard, but when the person went under and didn't resurface, I panicked and raced out."

"Saving me."

She tapped her fingers on the table, suddenly uncomfortable. "I didn't know it was you. I just knew someone was in trouble."

"That couldn't have been an easy swim."

"No, but I was terrified you were going to drown. I couldn't let it happen."

"You risked your life for a stranger."

"What is the point of being a strong swimmer if I can't save someone now and then?"

She'd deliberately kept her tone light, wanting to ease the tension.

He didn't smile. "I would have died without you."

"But you didn't. Now we just need to get your memory back, and all will be well." She gave him a bright smile and then rose, moving around the room, adjusting the shutters to give them more of the evening's breeze, and then taking her broom and sweeping out some sand that had found its way inside.

She could feel his gaze on her the entire time and it made her skin prickle and heat. She felt herself flush and her pulse quicken. He watched her the way surfers watched the waves—with focus and quiet intensity. It was unnerving and she suddenly wanted to adjust her skirt and gather her hair. She wanted to be pretty and worth the attention—

Josephine gave her head a shake.

She couldn't try to be someone she wasn't. She'd done that in the past, in Honolulu, for example, and it had been disastrous. "Judging from your accent," she said crisply, giving the threshold one last hard sweep of the broom, "you could be from Belgium, Luxembourg, France, Italy, Switzerland, Monaco, Sicily, Malta, Aargau—maybe even America. You've certainly managed to nail the American drawl."

He grimaced. "I don't feel American."

She returned the broom to the corner. "Then we can cross the States off the list." She did a quick count in her head. "Leaving nine possible cultures or nationalities."

"We're whittling down the list."

She laughed, and then her laughter faded as she studied the huge bruise still darkening his brow. "I just wish I knew how that happened," she said, nodding at his temple. "Were you injured in the fall? Did it happen before you went over the side?"

"I've wondered the same."

She studied his expression, debating if she should reveal her worries, but then he said what she'd been thinking, his voice deep, his delivery slow and thoughtful, "Because if it wasn't accidental—that would change everything, wouldn't it?"

CHAPTER TWO

HE DIDN'T KNOW his name. He didn't know where he was from. He didn't know what he did, or where he lived, or why he'd even be on a yacht "with friends." He didn't know if someone had meant him harm or if he'd simply had an accident and fallen overboard.

But there was one thing he did know, and it was this: he wanted her.

He woke thinking about Josephine and fell asleep thinking about her and it was all he could do to hide the physical evidence of his desire. He wasn't a boy. It shouldn't be difficult to control his hunger, but the fierceness of his desire made him wonder if he'd ever felt like this about anyone before or if this was typical of him. Desire. Hunger. Impatience.

Perhaps the intensity of the need was due to all the other unknowns.

He tried to distract himself with reading the books on the shelves in the house. When he was tired of reading, he swam or lay on the warm sand, soaking in the heat of the sun. But inevitably, as time passed, his thoughts turned to Josephine. He wanted to see her. He just wanted to be near her, so he'd pull a shirt on, one of the shirts from her father's closet that she'd lent him, and assist her with her work. He'd help with her notes, or he'd water the garden—anything if it meant he could be at her side, as he'd come to crave her shape, her scent, her smile.

She was beautiful and brilliant as well as innocent and earnest. He was certain she was a rare gem, a jewel among even the world's most beautiful women, and he said that to her one day, after they'd emerged from the sea following a swim.

She smiled at him, amused but also shy. "Thank you for the compliment, but seeing as you don't remember anything of your world, I'm not sure it's valid."

"I don't have to compare you to know that you're smart and kind. You're also cheerful and optimistic, and you make me happy. I have a feeling I'm not always easy to please."

"You certainly weren't cheerful on the beach with your friends. In fact, you were often quite aloof, sitting off on your own, staring out at the ocean. I would watch you and sketch you—"

"Sketch me?"

She nodded, blushing. "It's what I like to do when I have free time."

"I haven't seen you draw since I've been here."

"I do when you're not around, or late at night when you're sleeping."

"What do you draw?"

"This and that." Her blush deepened. "Mostly you."

He loved how her pink cheeks made her eyes look even more green. She was so fresh and pretty. She reminded him of a mermaid…a siren from the sea. "Why draw me?"

"You fascinate me."

"Why?"

"You have to know." Her lips pressed, her expression suddenly reminding him of a prim schoolteacher. "Don't make me spell it out."

He was enchanted by the line her full lips made and the firmness of her chin. His fingers itched to reach out and trace her pink cheek and the shape of her mouth. And just like that, his body hardened, the desire hot and insistent. "Apparently, my head injury has made me a little slow. Be kind and explain to me why someone like me would fascinate you?"

Her chin lifted higher. "I'll only tell you this one time."

"I'm listening."

"You're unbearably attractive—"

"Unbearably?"

"You're very intelligent."

"Can we get back to the unbearably attractive part? Is it possible to be *unbearably* attractive?"

"Yes. You've proven it. Let me continue." She

tapped her fingers as if counting her points. "You have a sense of humor—when you want to."

"I suppose that is a drawback, being unpredictable."

Her lips twitched. "You have rich friends. That yacht was enormous. But that's really more of a negative then a plus."

"Why a negative?"

"From an environmental standpoint, it's terrible."

"I agree."

Her brows arched. "You do?"

"I do. I'm always worried about the environment."

"You are?"

He nodded.

She frowned, a faint link forming between her eyebrows. "That's interesting," she murmured.

"Is it?"

Josephine nodded. "You're starting to have a clearer sense of self. I think some of your memories are returning. This is a good thing."

He felt a sudden wash of unease, and he didn't understand it. The return of his memory should be a great thing, and yet all he felt was a pervasive dread. "Let's talk about you instead."

"Why? I'm a boring academic—"

"Not boring, and academics are exciting."

She laughed. "Are they?"

"I went to school with brilliant women. There is nothing sexier than a smart woman—" he broke off as he realized what he'd said. He'd gone to school with brilliant women. And he knew he hadn't meant high school or grammar school. He'd meant university, and the words had been so comfortable, so natural. He also knew that calling university *school* was very American. Had he gone to school—college—in America?

He could see from Josephine's expression that she'd heard the reference, too, and understood it, as well.

"Your memory *is* returning," she said softly, breathlessly.

"You're healing me," he said. "All this sun and swimming."

She smiled back at him. "It's not as if there's a lot to do here. No TV or video games."

"But even if you had those, I don't think it's something you'd do. You love being outside. You're at home in the sea."

Her cheeks were pink, and her eyes were bright as she tucked a long strand of sun-streaked hair behind her ear. "I've always grown up next to the sea. First in Hawaii and then here. I can't imagine not swimming. If I go too many days without getting wet, I feel off. The sea always restores me."

"You are a fish."

She laughed. "My father says the same thing.

He says that I have scales and they dry out if I'm out of the water too long. Thus my close proximity to the beach."

"So maybe not a fish but a mermaid."

"Maybe," she answered, smiling, feeling strangely shy and sensitive because everything inside her seemed to be shifting and lurching. Changing.

She'd noticed it before, and she'd tried to suppress the feelings, but she couldn't pretend it wasn't happening, or real, any longer. She couldn't pretend that he wasn't aware of her. She couldn't pretend that there wasn't something taut and electric between them, because there was something about the way he looked at her, something in the intensity of his expression that made the air catch in her throat, making her heart gallop. The way he looked at her terrified her and yet, at the same time, thrilled her. Being near him was wonderful, confusing, exhilarating. No one had ever looked at her as if she were so important. No one had ever made her feel so beautiful. Every conversation made her feel alive, and she didn't know why because there was nothing terribly revealing said. And yet he fascinated her. He'd fascinated her on the beach when he'd been just a mysterious stranger, and her fascination only grew with every day because how could he—this gorgeous, handsome stranger— want her?

And yet, being wanted was doing something to her, seducing her, making her question everything she believed. She'd always thought that she'd never have sex with someone, not unless he was her forever love, the man who would marry her, the man who would share a life with her. Looking into his eyes, she figured she was losing out on something beautiful. This felt special. It felt like a once-in-a-lifetime opportunity, something she wasn't prepared to miss.

It helped that she knew the attraction wasn't one-sided.

It was clear from the heat in his gaze that he desired her, and the knowledge was a heady power. An aphrodisiac that made her restless and curious. He could make her feel so much with just a look. How would she feel if he touched her? *Kissed her?*

She didn't let herself think further than that. She'd never experienced more than a couple kisses, kisses that hadn't inspired her in any way, making her think there was no need to repeat the experience. Until now. Somehow she sensed that kissing her mysterious stranger would be entirely different. Maybe even life-changing.

But did she want that?

She looked hard at her stranger, who truthfully was no longer a stranger, but someone who was quickly becoming very important to her.

She'd spent so much of her life alone, or alone

with her father—which was virtually alone since he rarely spoke, his head always down, buried in his work. She understood her father's fascination with his work and his commitment to research, but every now and then she wanted…more.

She wanted to be seen.

She wanted to be known.

She wanted to be…loved.

Growing up as she had had taught her tremendous self-reliance, but there were times she felt that her life had also left her empty and aching for more. More connection. More expression. More emotion.

Usually these thoughts and feelings happened late at night, and she'd blame fatigue and the need to sleep.

But she was feeling these things almost constantly lately. The arrival of her mystery man had changed something within her.

His arrival had made her aware of the world out there and that there was more to the world than she knew. But even with that knowledge, she also knew she was happy on Khronos. Most of the time she wanted nothing but her work and the sun and the sea. Most of the time she was utterly content.

She needed to be content again.

Abruptly, Josephine rose, moving away, trying to escape the heat suffusing her skin and ache filling her chest. Her father had left her here to manage the foundation's station. She needed to stay focused on her responsibilities. "I'd better get back to work," she said huskily.

"Can I help?" he asked.

She shook her head. "I'm just going to check the solar panels. You relax—"

"That's all I've done the past few days. Show me what you're doing, or what needs to be done, so I can help while I'm here."

She smiled tightly. "Okay, follow me."

The old Greek cottage had been constructed of stones, without the charm of whitewash, and while it looked ancient and almost abandoned from the front, there were clean, well-maintained stairs behind—stairs that rose up to a clearing filled with a mass of solar panels and equipment, and another smaller stone house.

"That's where the foundation keeps all the seismic monitoring equipment. The equipment is connected to portable seismometers along the edge of the island, as well as some in the water. You see, we're sitting practically on top of a volcano. Khronos is just the tip, which is why we have the seismometers to detect rock movement in the earth's crust. Some movements may be the result of rising magma beneath the surface, which could mean an awakening volcano. We also have equipment here that monitors gases like sulfur dioxide, as an increase in sulfur dioxide could be an indication of magma near the earth's surface."

"And if that should happen? What do you do?"

"It hasn't happened in the past ten years, so I think I'm safe. Odds are, I'm safe."

"You're pretty nonchalant about something potentially catastrophic."

"Some people are terrified of volcanoes, particularly supervolcanoes, but there has never been such an eruption in human memory, and did you know there are actually quite a few people who choose to live near a volcano because they're drawn to the geothermal energy, the minerals and the fertile soil? I'm a fan of geothermal energy because it's very clean, and the resource is nearly inexhaustible.

"Speaking of energy, come see," she said, walking farther back along a compact dirt path that cut deeply through the rough, rocky terrain dotted with a few gnarled olive trees. "Twenty years ago the foundation was powered by those wind turbines before us. Unfortunately, they were prone to breaking down and the repairs were costly, and then new, improved solar technology became a better answer, so eventually no one bothered to repair or replace the turbines."

"They do look forlorn," he said, taking in the line of tall wind turbines that covered the top of the island.

"Luckily for us, solar works incredibly well, allowing the foundation to live completely off the grid. We use solar energy for almost everything. Light, heating, cooking, powering the radio—when the radio actually works—and now for desalination."

He'd been studying the solar panels, but she noted how his interest was piqued by the mention of their desalination system.

She walked him back to another frame, this one with its own set of panels, plus tubes, dials and black rectangular features, and motioned for him to crouch down beside her. "This is our baby and my personal favorite because this one gives us all our fresh water. In the beginning, we had to bring everything in, including gallons and gallons of water. We'd collect rainwater when we could, but if we had no rain, we'd begin to panic. Now, thanks to a partnership with my father's university, we're able to turn salt water into drinking water using only solar energy. Although there are over eighteen thousand desalination plants across the world, this one is unique in that it combines solar energy with brand-new technology allowing a family to generate enough clean water for individual use."

"How is it different from traditional desalination?"

"You're familiar with the desalination process?"

"Salt water is brought to a boil, creating steam. The steam is run through a condensing coil."

"Right. The traditional method is very energy inefficient and requires expensive, complex infrastructure. Over half of the cost of a distillation plant is spent on energy."

"So this is membrane distillation?"

She was impressed he knew that much. Perhaps he'd studied science in school, or something environment related. "Yes and no. The university took conventional membrane distillation, where hot salt water flows across one side of the porous membrane and cold freshwater flows across the other, and added in a layer of carbon-black nanoparticles. The carbon-black nanoparticles attract light, heating the entire surface of the membrane, converting as much as eighty percent of sunlight energy into heat, giving us more water with less energy. It's ideal for us with a compact footprint, but it will also revolutionize the way the world desalinates water because the nanoparticles are low-cost and commercially available."

"Fascinating," he murmured, studying the section with the nanoparticles and then the tubing where water dripped into a clear canister. "By integrating photothermal heating with membrane distillation you've created more productive and efficient technology."

"I haven't. The university program did. We're

lucky the scientists and engineers agreed to let us work with it here. We've had it eighteen months now and it's transformed our lives." She nodded toward the small garden off to the side. "Tomatoes, cucumbers, lettuce, carrots, and more. All possible now due to a never-ending supply of clean, drinkable water."

"I'd heard about an American university developing something like this, but it's amazing to see it in use here on Khronos and to know it's not just theoretical."

"It's a game changer for the world."

"Indeed," he murmured, and yet he wasn't looking at the system but rather at her; his gaze locked on her lips and she felt his scrutiny all the way through her.

Heat bloomed in her cheeks. She felt overly warm, her skin exquisitely sensitive, and she looked away, trying to hide how flustered she felt. She wanted his kiss and yet she feared it, too.

She wasn't experienced, and she knew most women her age would have had a number of significant relationships by now. She suddenly wished she'd had a more conventional life, a life where she'd had dates and boyfriends so she'd know what to do and how to respond.

She wanted to respond. Could he tell?

"You're bored," she said huskily, rising and brushing the coarse dirt from her hands.

"I'm not," he answered, rising, as well. "I'm fascinated by everything here. Not just by how you're managing to survive in the middle of nowhere but by you and this father of yours. I can't imagine any other father leaving his only daughter defenseless in such a remote spot."

"I'm not defenseless. I have the radio—" she broke off, lips tightening. Her heart was racing and her stomach churned and she felt close to tears and didn't know why. Nothing had happened, and yet somehow everything was happening and she seemed to be losing control. "Normally it works. I've never dropped it before. I've never broken it before. That accident was a fluke, just like you being here is a fluke. I've spent four years on Khronos and we've seen plenty of yachts, but none have ever stopped here before. And we've certainly never had any castaways, either—"

"Why are you afraid?" he asked, interrupting her torrent of words.

"I'm not." And yet her voice was high and thin, breathless.

For a long moment he was silent, studying her, and then he reached out and lightly traced her eyebrows, the right and then the left. Her breath caught in her throat as the touch sent sparks of hot sensation shooting through her veins. She stared at him, deep into his eyes, as he continued to explore her face, his fingertips light as they caressed the length of her nose, and then her cheekbone, and finally down along the line of her jaw.

"You are so beautiful," he murmured, his voice deep and rough.

She felt his voice and his touch all the way through her, an erotic rasp that teased her senses, making her skin flush and her body ache.

"No makeup, no designer clothes, no expensive blowouts. Just beautiful you," he added. "I didn't know women like you even existed."

"You say that now, but if you put me next to your lovely ladies from the yacht, you'd see how I'd pale in comparison."

"I don't think there is any comparison. You're extraordinary. Your mind. Your passion for your work. Your beauty. You're perfect."

"You're going to give me quite an ego."

"Good. You should know you're special. One in a million."

She drew back to look him in the face. He didn't turn away, letting her look, allowing her to see the flare of heat in his eyes.

"If you really feel that way, would you kiss me?" she whispered. "Unless that's not how you feel—"

"I've wanted to kiss you from the moment I opened my eyes and saw you in the room looking like an angel."

She swallowed hard. "I'm no angel," she murmured, even as her pulse beat double time, and her gaze drank him in, lingering on the hard, clean line of cheekbone and the shadow of a beard darkening his strong jaw. He shaved every morning, using her father's kit, but by late afternoon he had that shadow again. And then there was that mouth, his wide, firm mouth, his lips lovely. She'd loved drawing his face and loved his mouth most of all, wondering what it would feel like against her own. Wondering what he'd taste like. Wondering if kissing him would be different from kissing alcohol-fueled Ethan in Honolulu two years ago. That kiss had been so awful and sloppy that it had killed all desire to date.

He closed the distance between them, his hands circling her upper arms, bringing her in against him. His blue eyes glowed bright, the heat in the depths holding her, trapping her. Life seemed to slow, and the world shrank to just them.

Josephine could feel the thudding of her heart, and his hands wrapping around her arms, his skin so warm. She shivered at his heat and the way his hard chest pressed against her breasts, making her conscious that she was braless, and her nipples were tight and yet tender, and so sensitive to every breath he took.

This was what she wanted. This was all she wanted. Just to feel his mouth on hers…

His dark head dropped and very slowly his lovely, sensual mouth captured hers, sending sharp hot sparks of sensation through her. She heard a whimper and prayed it wasn't her. His hand rose to cup the back of her head, holding her still while his lips traveled over hers, teasing, tasting, discovering. She shuddered as more sparks of feeling shot through her, the heat making her melt on the inside, her brain flooded with wildly contradictory signals. She wanted more, so much more, even as another part whispered that she was out of his league.

"Second thoughts?" he murmured, lifting his head, his blue gaze meeting and holding hers.

"Um, yes. No. No." Because truly, she'd never felt so alive and so full of yearning about anything, but this was crazy. Her feelings were crazy. Excitement filled her veins, making her feel daring and wild…two things Josephine was not, nor ever had been.

And yet, it felt so good to feel excited and alive.

It felt so good to be touched and kissed.

"Tell me what you're thinking," he said, stroking her cheek, sending rivulets of fire through her, fire that she could feel in the tips of her breasts and deep between her thighs.

"Because it's obvious you're thinking."

"I know, and I'm sorry for it—"

"Don't be. Talk to me."

She drew a quick, shallow breath before blurting, "Do you think you could be married?"

"No."

"So you don't think you have a…a wife…somewhere?"

"No."

"How can you be so sure?"

His broad shoulders shifted. "Just the way I know I'm not American. It doesn't feel right. It doesn't sound right. It doesn't sound like…me."

He released her and she took a step back, and then another, not because she wanted to be apart from him but because she couldn't think when she was close to him and this conversation was important. "Your memory is returning."

"It must be."

"What sounds like you? Could you describe yourself? Who do you think you might be?"

"European. Wealthy." He grimaced. "Mediterranean, most likely. I think I run a company, or own my own company, and I'm good at it. I feel like I have quite a few employees, so my company can't be small. And I have a nagging suspicion that I'm a perfectionist, and, quite possibly, not easily pleased." He looked chagrined. "And if that is all true, I've just described a man that sounds like a pompous ass, which makes me despise myself, even though I don't yet know myself."

She laughed. "Considering that you don't know yourself, I think you're being a little hard on yourself. After spending the past few days with you,

I think you're a better person than you described. My gut says you're a very good person, as well as something of a loner, because even when you were with your friends, you were still a bit distant, and rather alone."

"Probably because I'm an unlikable prat—"

"No!" She interrupted with a throaty gurgle of laughter, and the sheer joy in the sound stopped her. Was that really her giggling? Sounding so impossibly girlish and happy? Josephine went through life very seriously. She was committed to facts, not feelings, and her life revolved around work and being useful and practical.

"What are you thinking now?" he asked.

"Is it that obvious I have a tendency to overthink everything?"

"I like it. I like you. Don't ever apologize for being you, Josephine."

The commanding gruffness in his voice made her throat swell closed. She felt a ridiculous need to cry. It had been such a strange and wonderful few days with him here, and everything inside her felt full and tender and new.

"We should head back to the house so I can focus on dinner," she said.

He caught her by the wrist to stop her from escaping. "You never answered my question. What were you thinking just a moment ago?"

She suppressed a shiver as he stroked the inside

of her wrist with the pad of his thumb, setting her alight. "That I'm happy," she said unsteadily, trying not to look at his mouth, trying not to remember their kiss earlier, because it had been perfect, and he made her feel beautiful and perfect, and standing close to him made her shockingly aware of how much she wanted to feel more. "And…" She gulped a breath and then lifted her chin, determined to finish her thought. "I'm happy you're here."

CHAPTER THREE

THE SKY WAS putting on a show tonight, the sunset a stunning orange on top of red, while waves crashed onto the beach—but the beauty was lost on him. Tension rolled through him. He didn't yet know himself, but he sensed parts of himself. It was strange and disorienting as well as infuriating. He didn't like not knowing himself, and he didn't want to be called by a name that wasn't his.

He wanted his name, and his identity.

He wanted to be himself, whoever that was, good or bad. He'd take the good and bad, fully embracing both because it was beyond frustrating to feel and think without a foundation of self, never mind self-knowledge.

Every time he heard himself say *I think*…a little voice inside him stopped him, questioning him. *Are you sure? How do you know?*

So, hurrah, his memory was returning, but it wasn't fast enough. He was impatient with the process. He didn't want pieces of himself; he wanted *all* his memory back. He wanted his life back. It wasn't enough to sense things about himself. He needed to *know*. He needed the truth.

The darkness inside him threatened to engulf him tonight and it crossed his mind that this life of hers was not him, which just made him want to know what his life was. He was by no means bored on Khronos, and he was enjoying being with Josephine, but this quiet island of hers wasn't his life.

He knew with certainty that his life wasn't quiet.

His work wasn't calm.

His world had stress and chaos and deadlines and people.

"Here," Josephine said, emerging at his side on the beach, a glass of wine in her hand. "I think you could use it."

He arched a brow.

"It's good wine," she said, smiling, her full lips curving, the sweet lift of her lips reminding him of their kiss earlier, and how soft her mouth had been beneath his, and how good she'd felt in his arms. Hunger stirred and he imagined doing all sorts of things to her that weren't innocent and would probably shock her.

But she'd enjoy it, and he'd enjoy her pleasure.

"And I need it because...?" he asked, smashing his hunger, not needing one more torment tonight.

"You're pacing this poor beach like a caged tiger. I'm hoping a couple glasses of Father Epi's merlot might help you relax."

He took the glass from her. "We've never had wine before."

"I don't normally drink, but this is a special occasion."

"Is it?"

She nodded, color suffusing her lovely cheek-bones. "I thought we should do something different tonight. Make tonight special. Hopefully it will provide some diversion and distract you from whatever is bothering you."

"You don't need to worry about me."

"But I do."

"Why?"

"I care about you." Her shoulders lifted and fell. "Which is why we're having dinner alfresco tonight. I've set a table for us and we will enjoy dinner outside and watch the sun set, and you'll be my first real date. Unless that is too awkward?" She bit into her lush lower lip for a moment, struggling with her confidence. "Am I horribly awkward? I'm afraid I am."

"There is nothing awkward about you," he answered huskily, reaching for her and drawing her close. "I would enjoy a dinner date with you very much, *bella*," he murmured, his head dropping to kiss her soft, warm mouth. For a moment she stiffened, and then in the next, she leaned into him, giving herself up to him. He traced the seam of her lips with his tongue and when her lips parted, he claimed her mouth, too, his tongue teasing hers, tasting her, wanting her. She shivered against him, and he kissed her jaw and then the side of her neck, feeling her shiver again as he kissed his way down to her collarbone, the air catching in her throat. She was so sensitive. He battled his desire, keeping his need in check.

She wanted a date. She wanted romance. He could do that.

"You don't have to do anything," she said quickly, breathlessly. "I'm taking care of the dinner and I've already set the table. Want to come see?"

He nodded because he did want to see, very much so. He offered her his arm, and she shyly tucked her hand through the crook of his elbow. They left the beach, returning to the little house, which looked altogether different with the glowing fire outside in a fire pit and a small round table covered with a vivid tablecloth with bright birds and butterflies against a black wool background. There were two place settings on the table, and tall tapered candles glimmered in the center. It was charming and rustic and he was touched that she had gone to such pains for him.

"That's not a Greek tablecloth," he said.

"No, it's from Peru. My dear Azucena made it for me before we left. I was supposed to save it for my hope chest—" She broke off when she saw his confusion. "Do girls not have hope chests where you're from?"

"I'm not sure. What is that?"

"It's where you save things for your wedding.

Linens and quilts and other things to help you begin your new home once you're married."

He noticed she wouldn't look at him as she talked, and color darkened her cheeks.

"I'm not planning on getting married," she added, moving around the table, adjusting the plates and glasses, "and it seems like such a waste to leave this lovely tablecloth in a chest forever, so I brought it out tonight. It's pretty, though, isn't it?"

"It is." But he wasn't looking at the cloth. He was looking at Josephine as the candlelight illuminated her profile. She'd changed at some point from her casual sundress into a long blue skirt that she'd paired with a white peasant-style blouse. Her long hair had been pulled into a loose knot that she'd attempted to secure with what looked like wooden sticks, but long tendrils of hair were slipping out and curling loosely at her neck and around her face.

Her cheeks were flushed and her eyes bright as she glanced at him, and her expression was nervous and shy, sweet and hopeful, and it was the hopefulness in her green gaze that made his chest tighten and ache.

He had a feeling his life was full of beautiful women, but none were like her. How could they be? Who could possibly be as smart and beautiful and yet also so capable? He marveled at her ability to make do with so little. She complained about nothing.

"Why won't you marry?" he asked, wanting to touch one of those long, loose tendrils that had slipped free from her chignon to rest on her smooth, tanned shoulder.

"It's just unlikely," she answered, giving him a smile. "It's not as if men wash up on my beach often."

"I did."

"Yes, but it took me eight years to rescue my first prince."

His brow creased. "Prince?"

She smiled, and a small dimple appeared near the corner of her mouth. "Like the story 'The Little Mermaid,' except I don't intend to give up my soul in order to marry or in order to make him—or anyone—happy."

"I confess, I don't know the story."

"How can you not know it?"

"I was an—" he stopped and looked away, perplexed. He'd come so close to saying *I was an only child.*

But was he?

And was that why he didn't know the story?

"It's not an American story," she added, "although Disney did a version of it. It's Hans Christian Andersen, and his stories are invariably really sad and depressing. I think they were meant to scare children into good behavior, but they gave me nightmares so my dad told my mom not to read them to me anymore, but of course I remember the ones that upset me most."

She glanced at him. "But no depressing conversation. Dinner is ready. Shall we eat?"

Josephine plated their dinner—roasted lamb fragrant with garlic, oregano, thyme, rosemary, and lemon juice. She loved cooking Greek food and tonight's lamb paired perfectly with the merlot and the sky, the stunning sunset fading to just a wisp of red and purple on the horizon.

He held her chair for her as she sat down, a chivalrous gesture that made her feel safe and protected. "Thank you," she murmured, watching as he took the seat opposite her, the candlelight reflecting off the bronze of his cheekbones and his inky-black hair. She felt a sizzle race through her as his blue gaze met hers and held. It was hard to think clearly when he made her feel so much, her pulse racing, her body humming with nerves and excitement.

She wanted him to kiss her again.

She wanted him to hold her and make her feel all the things she'd felt earlier, because this magic wouldn't last. He'd be gone before she knew it and this time here, together, would be just a memory. A memory she'd cherish forever.

"I can't imagine a more inviting table setting, or a more beautiful dinner companion," he said, lifting his wineglass. "To you, Josephine. Thank you for everything."

"It's my pleasure," she said, lightly clinking the rim of her goblet to his.

He sipped the wine and nodded. "This is really good wine."

"It's Greek, made by Father Epi in the monastic community Mount Athos. It's my father's favorite and what he always brings back with him."

"I'll have to remember it."

She felt her lips curve. "I'd rather you remember your name and those important things like where you live and what you do." Her smile faded. "Your family must be frantic. If you were mine, I'd be beside myself."

"It'd be nice to know who they are."

"I'm sure they are heartsick, as are your friends."

"Hmm."

She shot him a speculative look. "You don't think so?"

His jaw hardened, his gaze narrowing. "They didn't come back."

She'd thought the same thing many times. Carefully, she added, "Maybe they didn't know where you disappeared. It is a huge sea."

"Whoever I fought with knew I went overboard. Why didn't he sound the alarm?"

"If that person did know…you're still in trouble. That person is dangerous. He or she meant to do you harm. Otherwise the yacht would have circled back. Your friends, the rest of them, would never have left you."

"That's the first time, you said *he or she*." His gaze met hers and held. "Until now, you've always said *he*. Do you think it was a woman?"

"I don't know. I shouldn't have said anything. And I shouldn't speculate. I was never close enough to your group to hear conversations. I only watched from afar, and to be honest, I only really watched you." She felt her face go hot once again. Her shoulders twisted. She didn't know where to look. "You were the most interesting."

His gaze locked with hers and held, and what she saw in his eyes made the air bottle in her lungs and her skin heat. He wanted her, desired her, and it struck her for the first time that it wasn't because he was grateful she'd saved him—which was what she'd always told herself until now—but because he liked *her*, Josephine Robb, social misfit. It shouldn't matter that she could speak a half-dozen different languages but didn't know anything about popular American culture, but it did whenever she returned to the States. While women her age discussed fashion and the current social-media sensation, she felt foolish and exposed, a fish out of water.

It was all she could do to eat her dinner, and it was one of her favorite meals. Chewing, swallowing, talking, smiling became a challenge because she could feel him from across the table; she could feel his energy and it was dizzying. Her breasts peaked, her body felt hot, like liquid, and she pressed her knees together, trying to deny the sensitivity between her thighs.

"You've become very quiet," he said, as they finished their meal.

The candlelight flickered, casting a dancing shadow across his face. Her gaze followed the shadow and light as it moved over the slash of cheekbones, the strong forehead, the line of his nose, and the utterly masculine jaw. He was handsome and virile but also hard, with a toughness, a fierceness, at his center that made her think she wouldn't ever want to be his adversary. Far better to have him in her corner, on her side.

"I should clear the table," she said huskily.

"No, you shouldn't," he answered, his gaze focused intently on her.

She felt her mouth tingle beneath his scrutiny, and her face warmed, the skin feeling taut and sensitive. The heat in his blue eyes took her breath away, making her heart pound. Awareness rippled through her, desire coiling low in her belly with a need and a desperation she'd never felt until now. He'd awakened something within her that made her restless, even frantic.

She didn't just want him; she needed him.

There might never be another who made her feel this way. Beautiful and valuable. Excited and alive.

"Come here," he said, leaning back in his chair.

He didn't extend a hand, nor were the words sharp or frightening, but the command was undeniable. He expected her to go to him. He knew she'd obey.

And she knew it, too.

She rose on shaky legs and walked around the small table to his side.

His dark head tipped, and his gaze slowly traveled over her, from her hot flushed cheeks to her full mouth and down over her shoulders. His attention riveted on the tips of her breasts pressing against the thin gauze of her blouse, and then finally moved down over her waist and hips.

The hunger in his eyes made her tremble. She wasn't frightened, and yet the heat in her body now seemed to center low, pooling in secret places that made her damp. She felt as if he was slowly turning her to wine and honey.

"I want you," he said, and his deep voice had a rasp in it that made her nipples tighten. "But I'm trying to be respectful," he added. "I'm aware of how much I owe you—"

"No."

"I do. I owe you my life."

"Then don't want me. Not if it's because you're grateful. I don't want to be wanted out of some misguided gratitude—" She broke off as he reached out and pulled her down onto his lap, his hands locking around her waist.

"I don't want you out of gratitude. I want you because I can't sleep at night anymore because my body aches for you. I want to touch you and taste you and be in you. The only reason I've held back is because you're innocent. I'm hoping to God you're not, because then I wouldn't feel like such a bastard for wanting to take you and make you mine."

Her thighs clenched as heat ricocheted through her, the desire as sharp as a razor's edge.

"Tell me you're not a virgin. Tell me this wouldn't be your first time." His gaze, so hot, blistered her, while his deep voice scratched her senses, gravel-rough.

"It would be my first time," she answered unsteadily, "but everyone has to have a first time. Why can't it be with you?"

"Because I don't think I'm good for you. I don't think I'm what you need."

"How do you know that?"

"I don't."

"*Exactly.* We don't know very much of anything except that I'm as attracted to you as you are to me, and I like how you make me feel. I like this, whatever this is, between us and I want more of it, not less."

His jaw flexed, hardened, just as she could feel him harden beneath her bottom in undeniable proof of his desire. His erection made her feel even more sensitive and she exhaled in a rush, overwhelmed by the sensation coursing through her. "I want you," she said thickly, sliding her hands up his chest, exploring the hard, warm plane of muscle. "I want you to be my first."

Her words were like gasoline on an open flame.

He wanted to strip her bare right there and feast on her. He wanted his mouth on every inch of her. He wanted her, oh, so very wet and writhing beneath him.

He could make her squirm and shudder and cry out his name.

If he were a gentleman, he'd release her, push her off his lap and tell her to go to bed.

He'd go for a swim to cool off and he'd swim until he burned off this terrible need.

If he were a gentleman, he'd wait for her to fall asleep before he returned to her father's room where he slept every night.

But he wasn't a gentleman. He didn't know very much about himself, but he knew that much.

Head dropping, his lips brushed hers, not because he was being careful with her but because he was feeling cruel.

He wanted her to ache for him.

He wanted her to crave him the way he craved her, and so he teased her lips and teased her with touches that were light and unsatisfying, his caress brushing her shoulders, the sides of her breasts, the outside of her hip, every touch designed to make her arch and flex, her slim back a bow drawn taut.

She was breathing harder now, short gasps, and her mouth lifted, trying to find his. She wanted his kiss. She wanted him.

He grazed the pebbled nipple of one breast with the back of his knuckles, a fleeting touch that made her whimper and her body gyrate on his lap. Her eyes were cloudy, the pupils so dilated her eyes looked almost black now.

He brushed the other just to make her dance again, and she did.

He nearly growled with pleasure. She was his.

Finally he took her mouth, his lips claiming her, his hunger barely leashed. As he took her mouth, he drank in her groan of pleasure. Her mouth was both hot and cool. She tasted fresh and impossibly sweet, and as his tongue traced the seam of her lips, her mouth opened to him. His tongue plunged in, sweeping, stabbing, punishing.

He didn't know why he wanted to punish her. She was nothing short of heaven, an angel here on earth.

Maybe that was why he was angry—and not with her, but with himself.

He didn't deserve her.

He shouldn't take her.

He shouldn't be the one to steal her innocence. For God's sake, she'd kept a hope chest, filled with desires and dreams and hopes, and tonight she'd brought out a special tablecloth, and now he was going to take her virginity?

He shouldn't do this, he shouldn't. He didn't even know if there were other claims on him. He didn't think he was married—he wore no ring; there was no tan line—but could he have a significant other waiting for him somewhere? Worrying about him?

Missing him?

He broke off the kiss and lifted her, putting her on her feet before walking away, putting distance between them so he couldn't reach her easily.

For a moment the only sound was the crackle of the fire and the hum of the ocean as waves broke on the shore.

The rising moon cast a pale glow and he knew if he turned, he'd see her where he'd put her. She hadn't moved. She stood frozen, staring at him, waiting.

Wondering.

"I can't do this," he ground out. "I can't just take your innocence because I want to. It's wrong, at every level."

"Not even if I give you permission?" she said.

He heard the wobble of hurt in her voice and he glanced over his shoulder to see that yes, she was exactly where he'd left her. She looked rooted to the spot, except she no longer glowed. Her lips were pressed together and she looked pinched. Wounded.

And he'd done that to her, as well.

Pain twisted within him and he hated himself for putting her through this. He ought to know better. He was a man, not a boy.

"You should be protected," he said roughly. "It's what your father would want for you, and what you need. I can't just wash up on your beach and claim you—"

"Why not? Why not if it's what I want?" The bruised tone was gone, replaced by something stronger, fiercer. "I'm twenty-three, almost twenty-four. This isn't the Middle Ages. I am not a ward, and I do not belong to a man. I can decide for myself what is best for me."

He laughed, the sound mocking and unkind. "And you think I'm best for you?"

Her chin notched up. "I think you can teach me what I want to know."

He lifted a brow. "Teach you?"

"As you can tell, I haven't had a lot of experience. I've actually had almost no experience. There have been kisses," she added flatly, "and some uncomfortable groping, but that is all. As you can see there are not a lot of men here, and I'm happy here, so I'm relatively...untutored...when it comes to sex. Which is why I want you to be my first so I won't feel so...foolish...the next time."

The next time.

Her words flamed his temper. Primal emotion flooded him, making his blood boil and his shaft throb and ache.

He hated the idea of her with anyone else. He hated to think of any man touching her.

"You say you owe me your life," she added, her winged brows arching higher, as imperious as a queen. "Well, I don't want your life. I just want you to bed me. I want you to show me how it is between a man and a woman so that I can be confident in the future. It would help me feel less awkward when I have sex in the future."

"You keep calling it sex. Why not lovemaking?"

"Because I'm a scientist and haven't been raised with euphemisms."

"But when you're with someone you truly desire, it's not just sex—it's bigger and more powerful. Transformative, if you will."

"Would it be that way with us?"

"If it's right."

"And if it's not?"

"It would feel like two bodies touching, rubbing, with hopefully a release in there somewhere."

"Sex can be bad, then?"

"With the wrong person, yes. With the wrong person it can be disconcerting."

"Even for a man?"

"It's a profoundly intimate act. I always enjoy it best in the context of a relationship."

"Ah." Her head nodded once, a thoughtful movement. "That's why you don't want to do it with me. We have no relationship. It wouldn't satisfy you."

"On the contrary, we have a very unique relationship, and making love to you is all I've thought about these past few days. But if I were to take you to my bed, I'm not sure I could, or would, let you go."

"Then don't," she answered simply.

For a moment they stood where they were, just looking at each other, the crackle of the fire mimicking the crackle of heat in his veins, making his shaft longer and harder, making him ache for her.

She patted the chair he'd left. "Come back here," she said coolly.

It wasn't a plea but a command, just as he'd commanded her earlier.

"Come sit down again and let me sit with you, like we were," she added. "Let us see how this goes without your conscience telling you things. I have a conscience of my own. I don't need yours deciding what I want or need. I can and will do that for myself."

He'd found her innocence seductive, but this version of Josephine was far sexier and even more compelling.

He sauntered toward her, aware of how her gaze

boldly moved over him, giving him the same thorough examination he'd given her earlier, before her attention focused on his hips and the rigid length of him thrusting against the fabric of his trousers.

The tip of her tongue touched her lips and he wanted to roar with need and lust. She might be innocent and yet she had a sensual nature which called to him, stirring him. He took his seat and leaned back in the wooden chair, his brow lifting, challenging her. "Your Highness?" he taunted lowly.

She sat down on his lap, legs together, facing him. "Now what?" she whispered.

He didn't answer her with words. Instead he drew her arms behind her back and wrapped one hand around both of her wrists, holding her captive and still. He liked her like this—helpless and his. He liked how her breasts jutted and her lips parted, her breath coming fast.

He kissed the corner of her mouth, and then her mouth, feeling how her lips quivered against his.

He licked at her lower lip, his tongue finding all the nerve endings inside. She wriggled on his lap, hips rocking, and he longed to reach down and rub her between her thighs. Part of him wanted to shock her, while another part wanted to soothe her. She was passionate and responsive and utterly gorgeous…and right now she was his, all his.

"Can you feel me?" he growled, kissing the side

of her neck, his teeth scraping across her skin. "Can you feel me between your thighs?"

She nodded her head, a jerky nod, even as his tongue flicked her tender earlobe and then swirled inside the shell of her ear, making her groan.

"I can feel you," he murmured, tugging on her hands, drawing them lower so that he held her hands against her butt, making her back arch even more. Her white cotton blouse clung to her small, high breasts, the thin fabric outlining her nipples. His head dropped and he sucked on one nipple, drawing on it hard.

She gasped, and whimpered, grinding down against him. He could feel her through his trousers, her body hot, wet.

With his free hand he worked the blouse off one shoulder, revealing the simple white cotton bralette, the thin fabric cup damp from his mouth. He stroked the pebbled nipple, making her squirm again.

"I can feel your heat and your need," he said, his lips just below her ear. "You are so wet, and it's so sexy."

She shuddered at his words.

"What I want to do with you is very hot and rather indecent. I'm afraid it would shock you."

She was finding it increasingly hard to breathe. "How so?"

"I would like to touch you, everywhere, and

discover with my hands and my mouth what you enjoy. I'd like to kiss you between your thighs and use my tongue to make you come—"

"Would you enjoy that?" she asked, interrupting him.

He laughed softly at her wrinkled nose, her expression indicating disbelief.

"I would like it very much."

"You're telling me the truth?"

"I will always tell you the truth. No lies between us. It would ruin everything."

She stared deep into his eyes. "I do trust you," she said quietly, firmly, as if giving him reassurance. "Which is why I want you to be my first. You're supposed to be my first. I've been waiting for you."

"As much as I like the sound of that, I'm afraid it doesn't make sense."

"But it does. It's science," she said, "the laws of something or other. Nature or physics. If I could think clearly, I could tell you why it's meant to be, but I can't think clearly, not with you kissing my neck and everywhere else. You're clouding my rational brain."

"I should stop."

"No. You should most definitely not stop." She drew her head back down to his, kissing him sweetly, persuasively. "Promise me?"

"Promise," he answered, rising with her in his

arms. As he walked, he kissed the side of her neck, making her breath catch in her throat. He was already hard and hungry, but that faint hitch in her breath made his body burn and throb.

She was gorgeous and sensitive and she made him feel so many good things. He wondered if he'd ever felt like this before. He couldn't imagine desiring anyone as much as he desired her.

He headed to the stone house, hesitating in the center room, not sure which way to go. Josephine pointed to her room. Her bed was small, considerably smaller than her father's, but it would still be plenty big enough for the two of them.

In her room, he sat down on the edge of the low bed and drew her between his thighs. His hands ran up and down her sides, stroking the length of her, savoring the feel of her. She was slim and toned and yet she had lovely curves, perfect breasts and generous hips, and a firm backside that was meant to be touched.

"What do I do?" she whispered as he reached for the hem of her blouse.

"Nothing. Let me," he answered, lifting her blouse up and then untying her sarong so that the fabric fell to the ground. Next to go was the plain white bralette and matching white panties, and once they were off, she was his, and beautifully bare. He smothered his groan of appreciation. "You are so beautiful," he said, drawing her before rising up and shifting her back on the bed and slowly extending his body over hers, covering her.

Her arms wound around his neck, her fingers at his nape.

"Kiss me," she whispered.

And he did.

Josephine closed her eyes at the hunger in his kiss. His lips were firm and the pressure of his mouth parted her lips. She shuddered at the feel of his hand under her breast and then on her breast, fingers stroking the tight, peaked nipple, sending rivulets of feeling throughout her body. Her hips pressed up against his, his thick shaft extended across her belly. She'd always wondered what this would be like, and he was right; she'd imagined it as a clinical sort of thing, but there was nothing clinical in the heat and texture and sensation.

He made her feel so wonderfully alive. She couldn't imagine this moment with anyone else, just him.

He lifted his head to gaze down at her. There was something in his expression that made her chest tighten and her heart thump with pain.

"You promised," she whispered. "You promised you wouldn't stop. And I won't regret this, I swear to you." She caressed his neck and then her hands went to his shoulders. "Don't be afraid."

He laughed low, as though amused. "I'm not

even closer to kiss one pink-tipped breast. Her nipple puckered, tightening as his lips brushed the sensitive tip.

His body throbbed all over again, his erection straining against the zipper of his trousers. His tongue swept the peak lightly before his mouth closed over the damp tip. She shuddered as he drew on the nipple, her slim back arching. His hands settled on her hips, holding them firmly, thumbs stroking her hip bones.

She practically danced in place, making soft little whimpering sounds. She was so sweet, so innocent, and he battled to keep his desire in check, not wanting to rush.

The first time was special. The first time should make her feel good and beautiful.

He kissed his way to her other breast, giving the dark pink nipple the same attention and then some, pulling harder on the tip, working it and feeling how her body responded, hips rocking harder, her legs now trembling.

He stroked down her hips and then to her outer thighs and back again. He stroked lightly, awakening every nerve he could as her breath became increasingly shallow. She was practically panting as he caressed up the inside of her knee, up her smooth taut thigh to tease the curls between her legs. But instead of touching her then, he caressed back down her thigh and then up so that his knuckles grazed her. She bucked a little against his hand as he trailed a finger where she was most sensitive.

She was trembling against him now, her hands on his shoulders, holding her up. He slipped a hand between her thighs, finding her slick folds. She was so tender, so warm, so wet. He desperately wanted to put her on the bed and part her thighs and lick her, and taste her, but he didn't want to overwhelm her. This was clearly all so new to her, and so he contented himself with stirring her and heightening her senses and her pleasure. He wanted her fully aroused to make sure her first time was as comfortable as possible.

She shuddered again when his fingertips traced her delicate lips and then her nub. Her breath even shuddered as he stroked her, oh, so lightly there.

"I can't stand anymore," she said lowly, hoarsely.

"Sit. Switch places with me," he said.

Her expression was uncertain and yet she did as he asked, and he used the moment to strip off his clothes before kneeling in front of her, his hands circling her ankles. He stroked the fine bones in her ankles and then up over her shins and calves to her knees, and then down again, working the backs of her calves. He could feel her relax, her breath grow deeper and slower. Gradually, he shifted his attention higher on her legs, stroking up her thighs and down again, and with each stroke he pressed her legs back, opening them gradually to him. She

stared at him, fascinated, her husky breath the only sound in the dark room.

The moon wasn't yet high enough to see her well, but he could see enough to be painfully aroused—pale skin, her thick honey-brown hair tumbling over one shoulder and breast, and the triangle of curls at her thighs. She gleamed in the dim light, her long limbs exquisite, her small, full breasts perfect. He felt beyond hungry; he was ravenous and he wanted to feast on her. Instead he was careful, and he leaned between her thighs to press a tender kiss in the hollow where her thigh connected to her pelvis. She groaned softly as he blew lightly on her inner thighs, focusing the air on her curls. She jerked against his hold, her breath hitching again.

"This is a kind of torture," she murmured.

"The best foreplay always is," he answered, parting her there to slip his fingers across her. She was hot and so tender, her soft flesh like liquid velvet. He kissed her on her nub, then used the tip of his tongue across her.

She shivered and cried out.

His body went rock hard, so hard he felt as if he'd pop out of his skin. He wanted her, wanted to be buried in her sweet wet heat, buried so deeply that they were one, forever one, making her his, and only his. He kissed his way back to the junction of her thighs, kissing her lightly, soothing her afraid, and I'm glad you're not afraid, either. The first time isn't always comfortable, but it'll get better."

"I've heard that, too."

He kissed her, smiling against her mouth, and then his smile faded as the kiss turned hot and electric. She opened her legs for him, allowing his hips to settle between her thighs. He entered her slowly, taking his time, and Josephine had to draw a deep breath and tell herself to relax when it began to pinch and then burn, and then there was all that fullness and that pressure inside her, so different from anything she'd ever felt before. He was right. It wasn't comfortable and she wondered how anybody enjoyed this.

He must have sensed her panic, because he held still and kissed her, biting and then sucking on her lower lip, distracting her from everything but his teeth and tongue. Gradually the sting eased and the pressure was less overwhelming. He rocked his hips a little, shifting inside her, and as he eased out and then in, she found herself holding her breath again, but this time because it was a strange fluttery sensation that felt new but good.

"Do that again," she urged.

He laughed softly. "Many, many times," he answered, withdrawing again to thrust in more deeply. The fluttery good feeling happened again and continued with every thrust, and the pleasure built, the sensation erotic, making her arch and dig her heels into the mattress of the bed.

He met the lifting of her hips with a deeper, harder thrust, and the pleasure continued to rise, pressure and pleasure swirling, tightening so that she felt almost dizzy from it. She didn't know what she was waiting for, or reaching for. She just knew he couldn't stop, and she wanted whatever it was that he was doing and making her feel. Emotion and sensation joined together, hot and intense, as she tried to grip him with her body, wanting to keep him inside her where he felt so good, but he wouldn't be stopped and her skin grew hot and damp, and she felt the heat sweep through her, her skin prickly and tingling all over.

She panted with the need and tension, her body wound up, too wound up, and she didn't know what to do or where to go with the tension, and then he reached down, between them, and touched her where she was so very sensitive, circling her nub even as he drove into her, and his touch there, as he thrust deep inside her, made her shatter. She stifled her cry by pressing her mouth to his chest, but the waves of pleasure didn't stop. The climax continued, hard and intense, breaking her into a million shimmering pieces. She felt like stardust strewn across the sky and it was earth-shattering, heart-stopping.

Even as she was still floating like stardust, her

mind so scattered, she felt him groan and stiffen, his hoarse guttural cry not so different from her own.

Josephine's arms tightened around him and she held him fiercely, desperately thinking her life would never be the same.

It could never be the same.

He would forever be a part of her now because she had just given him a piece of her heart.

He woke up in the night and glanced around, wondering what had woken him, and then he realized it was the moonlight streaming through the window, falling across the bed in white streaks of light.

The moonlight illuminated Josephine's elegant profile. Her features were delicate and refined, reminding him of a fairy-tale princess. Every day he discovered something new about her, and tonight he'd discovered her passion. Part of him felt guilty for taking her virginity, and yet another part of him agreed with her—they were meant to be. Destined to be together. She was beautiful and brilliant, innocent and earnest, and temptingly sweet.

His head dipped and he pressed a light kiss to her temple and then another to her cheek.

She stirred and moved closer to him, her slim warm body pressed to his. "What's wrong?" she murmured sleepily.

He stroked her long silky hair back from her cheek. "Nothing."

"You're awake."

"The moon woke me."

"I'll close the curtain."

"No, don't. Then I couldn't see you, and I want to see you."

Her lips curved, her cheeks rising with her soft smile.

He dropped another light kiss on her lips. "You're a jewel, Josephine. A rare jewel."

Still smiling, she nestled even closer so that her cheek rested on his chest. "Thank you for the compliment, but seeing as you don't remember anything of your world, I'm not sure it's valid."

"Let me be the judge of that."

"Yes, my lord," she said with a faint laugh, her breath a light caress against his bare chest, and then she fell back asleep, and he lay awake for another hour, just holding her and watching the big full moon high in the sky.

This wasn't his life, or his world, but in some ways he was quite certain it was the best life he'd lived, as well as the best world.

Josephine woke the next morning and stretched and smiled as she felt his arm tighten around her. He was here. It wasn't a dream. She was so glad because it had been the best night of her life.

She slipped from bed and pulled on her bikini and then headed outside for an early-morning swim. As she swam she heard the buzz of a helicopter. It was far from the beach, but the hum grew louder. She stood up in the water, hands over her head, waving frantically as the helicopter moved toward her and then headed in a different direction, flying away.

She ran back toward the house. He was just leaving her bed, pulling on the pair of her father's shorts she'd given him along with the other clothes. The shorts were huge and so he anchored them with a belt as he raced back outside with her.

"It came so close," she said, running toward the beach. "And I waved, and I thought it must have seen me but then it went away."

"Maybe it did see you. Maybe it's gone for help."

"Maybe."

They spent the rest of the day on tenterhooks waiting for the helicopter to return or a glimpse of a boat, but the morning turned into afternoon, and then dusk fell. "I'm sorry," she said to him where they sat side by side on the sand.

"I'm not," he answered, turning his head to look at her. "I'm glad. This gives me more time with you. It gives me more time to discover you and all the different ways I want to know you."

"But we made love."

"There are so many ways to make love."

She chewed her lip, hiding her smile. He made her feel so excited and nervous and shy and hopeful and all those emotions kept rising in her, bubbling up, making it impossible not to smile.

"You like that," he said, his voice dropping, growing husky.

She blushed, even as her smile stretched wider. She shouldn't smile. She shouldn't encourage him, and yet she loved how he made her feel and how amazing it had been to be his last night. His weight, his scent, his heat…the friction and the pleasure.

"I did," she said unsteadily. "I loved it. I loved being with you. It was…perfect."

"And that was just the beginning," he answered, drawing her toward him, pulling her on top of him as he lay back. She felt him beneath her, hard and warm, his chest crushing her breasts, and his erection pressed to the apex of her thighs, the heavy rigid length making her impossibly aware of his desire. His hands shifted from her waist to her hips and then lower, to cup her butt, his hands so warm on her that she felt as if she was melting.

He cupped the back of her head, kissing her deeply, making her whimper with need. She wiggled against him, her hips dancing over him, encouraging him, practically begging him to take her.

She wanted him to fill her and stretch her. She wanted the maddening pressure and then the explosive release. She wanted everything he'd shown her last night, and even more wild and fierce tonight.

Passion—she wanted the passion he'd awoken within her.

And then he was lifting her and he was sliding lower, holding her thighs apart until he settled beneath her, his face under her most private place.

She pressed against his shoulders, trying to escape, but he held her knees firmly, keeping them wide-open so that he could her kiss there, between her thighs. She shuddered and swallowed a cry.

"Take your bikini bottoms off," he told her. "Now."

It was a definite command but also unbelievably sexy, and she peeled them off, trying not to panic. This was what she wanted—him. Them. Earlier today she'd wanted him to want her like this; she'd wanted him to show her all the things she didn't know, and he could, she thought. He could teach her and share with her, helping her discover the world that lay beyond Khronos's beach.

"Come here," he growled. "Kneel over me."

She'd wanted to be daring; she'd wanted to take risks but this was terrifying. "I'm not sure—"

"I am. I want you. I want to taste you again. Last night was not enough."

Heat rushed through her, heat and need and fear that perhaps this was all a dream and once she opened her eyes, he'd be gone.

And then his mouth touched her there, and his

tongue found her between the slick folds, and she cried out as he stroked her and sucked on her, drawing the sensitive nub between his lips and then his teeth, tugging and licking until she felt as if she'd explode out of her skin.

He slipped a finger inside her, finding more sensitive spots as he sucked on her, and she couldn't fight the intense waves of pressure and pleasure building. She screamed as she climaxed, and the orgasm shuddered through her, making her body writhe and bend.

He lifted her up and turned her around so that she lay in the sand, and he stretched out over her. She stared up at him, so dazed she could barely focus.

"You liked that," he murmured, pushing her hair back from her face.

"You could say that," she whispered, reaching up to tug on his shirt. "But I'm feeling greedy. I want you. I want what we did last night. That was heaven. Please take this off. Your shorts, too."

"We have to be careful," he said. "I wasn't careful enough last night. I didn't pull out fast enough."

She struggled to follow what he was saying and then she understood. Careful as in careful not to get her pregnant. Careful as in birth control. "Oh. Right. Smart." Why hadn't she thought of any of that?

But then, there was no time for thinking about anything, not when he was settling over her, handsome and naked and beautiful. She'd never met anyone half so beautiful. And then he was kissing her again and lowering himself to cover her before he entered her, his thick shaft stretching her and filling her so that her breath caught and she had to relax to accommodate him.

But then when he began to move, slowly, the uncomfortable sensation eased, and the pressure became a good pressure as he found the spot inside her that liked being touched. "Again," she said, lifting her hips. "Do that again and again."

He laughed softly against her neck. "My pleasure."

And then she didn't want to talk anymore, not when she was feeling so much heat and sensation and emotion.

With him, like this, she felt beautiful. Together with him, like this, everything was perfect.

The days passed, one after another. The sun shone brightly every day, long hot days that only cooled in the late afternoon as the wind blew. They spent most of their time together. He felt guilty that she wasn't working very much, but he knew that it was just a matter of time, too, before her father would return and everything would change. Maybe that was why he couldn't get enough of Josephine, craving her body and warmth. Or maybe he couldn't get enough because she felt like sunshine and life—

so open and warm and affectionate. Her smile did something to him, creating strange pain and pressure in his chest. He feared what he didn't know, and yet it only served to make the present even more important. It made *her* more important. He wasn't going to lose her, either. She was his. She belonged with him. He knew that much.

"My father should be back very soon now," she said, curling up against him late one afternoon, her hand on his chest, her fingers lightly caressing his skin. He loved the way she touched him. It felt right. She felt right in his arms, in his bed. "Just three days, and when he returns, he will know who to contact," she added, "and what to do."

The news should please him. Obviously, he knew they could not remain like this forever. But he dreaded reality, unable to fathom the future or the truth of it all when he was so removed from it here with her.

She misinterpreted his silence, because she looked up at him, giving him one of her radiant, reassuring smiles, which never failed to put an ache in his chest. "My father will like you. Very much."

He couldn't answer her smile, not when there was so much heaviness within him. "There is a whole world out there that we don't know."

"But we will discover it together, yes?"

He kissed her brow and then the tip of her small, straight nose and then, finally, the lushness of her lips. Almost immediately desire flared, the warmth of the kiss sparking hot cravings. He pulled her closer, wanting to lose himself in her rather than at the edge of the unknown. The unknown wasn't his friend. But she was. Here on Khronos, she was his world. She was his everything.

"I love you," she whispered, as he entered her, thrusting deep.

He didn't say it back, but then, he didn't think she expected him to.

Later that night, he woke up and glanced toward the windows, looking to see if it was light. But there wasn't a wall of windows where he expected glass to be. The window was on a different side of the room, and it was a simple square window with a simple grid in the middle.

He frowned. This wasn't his room. This wasn't his home.

He swung his legs out of bed. The ground was very close. It jarred his knees. His bare feet arched against the roughly cobbled floor. Why was he here? He didn't belong here. He lived somewhere grand. He lived somewhere…

His throat worked. He swallowed as the past returned, colliding with the present, because he *knew*.

He knew his name. Alexander.

He knew who he was. He knew what he was.

Alexander glanced around the room, under-standing where he was. Not in Aargau but in Greece, on this island with Josephine who'd res-cued him.

He looked over and there she was, still sleep-ing in the bed. Her bed. Her cottage. Her island, not his.

Her long honey hair spilled across her bare shoulder. Her thick lashes rested on her cheek. She was stunning even in her sleep. His very own mermaid.

She'd saved him. He would have died—drowned—if not for her, and then when he was still weak, she'd taken care of him. And then last night she'd told him she loved him, and he hadn't answered her with words, but he'd shown her how much her faith in him mattered to him by making love to her for hours, worshipping her body since something inside him kept him from giving her his heart.

He'd thought that maybe he couldn't give him-self to her fully because he didn't know who he was. It was what she'd said, and he'd hoped maybe it was true, but now he knew why he couldn't love her. Because she wasn't his, and he wasn't free.

He was Prince Alexander Julius Alberici of Aar-gau, and he was betrothed to another.

CHAPTER FOUR

HE NEEDED TO tell her.

Alexander needed to tell her that his memory had returned, that he knew who he was.

But he also knew that once he did, everything would change. Forever.

He wasn't ready to lose her. He wasn't ready to lose the warmth of what they had. He'd never felt like this with anyone, and he'd never been wanted like this by anyone. She didn't even know who he was, or what he was, and yet she wanted him.

And so that day, all day, he watched her, paying attention to everything, committing to memory the sunlight on her hair and how it illuminated her stunning profile. He watched her walk and that way she'd almost skip because of the joyous bounce in her step. She was so buoyant, so happy, she radiated light and goodness.

Hope and strength.

He hadn't been raised with women like her. He hadn't ever known that women like her existed. His mother had been born a princess and had been raised strictly, taught to be conscious and vigilant about the image she presented, conscious of her elevated place in society. Lovely Josephine was nothing like his mother. She was free and lacked conceit and arrogance. She was humble and practical and so quick to smile and laugh.

He'd dated many women over the years but there had never been anyone like Josephine.

And his fiancée, Princess Danielle, was nothing like Josephine, either.

The heavy rock returned to his stomach, the weight reminding him that his past and future were about to collide and it would be painful and ugly.

No, he couldn't think of the future now—it wasn't here. And he couldn't dwell on Princess Danielle, either.

He didn't want to think of anything but Josephine, acutely aware that they were on borrowed time and that the real world would intrude soon, and once it did nothing would ever be the same.

"What's wrong?" Josephine asked, coming up behind him to wrap her arms around his neck. She leaned against him, kissing his cheek, her body so warm against his back. She smelled of sunshine and lavender and the honey-vanilla-scented shampoo she used on her hair. "Is your head hurting again?"

Not his head, he thought, but his conscience.

He'd spent the past week making love to her, promising her the future, even as another woman counted down the weeks, anticipating their wedding in the Roche Cathedral across from the Alberici palace. He was going to end up hurting one if not both of them. He reached up to cover one of Josephine's hands. "My head is fine," he answered quietly. "I just keep thinking about the future."

"It won't be so bad," she said, her voice gentle.

She was always so gentle with him, so patient. As if he deserved tenderness and patience when he was anything but tender and kind himself.

She wouldn't like who he was, he thought.

She wouldn't like Prince Alexander Julius at all.

The emotion was intense and uncomfortable, so uncomfortable that he couldn't allow himself to go there. Instead, he pulled her down onto his lap and kissed her, his hand fisting in her thick hair, warm from the sun.

But kissing her only made the emotion hotter and fiercer. He didn't want to let her go. There was no way in hell he wanted to lose her—she was the first woman he'd ever needed, ever craved—but at the same time, Alexander didn't know how he'd reconcile his duty and responsibility to his kingdom and Princess Danielle with his feelings, and Alexander knew too well that in his world feelings didn't matter. Feelings, in fact, were inconsequential. What mattered was fulfilling one's duty.

He'd tell her tomorrow, he vowed, breaking off the kiss. Her green gaze met his and held. She looked at him with such trust, such love. His chest tightened, guilt pummeling him. He'd never been dishonest with anyone before. How could he hurt her? How could he do this to her?

She wouldn't stand in the way of his wedding to Danielle, either. She'd tell him to do the honorable thing. She wouldn't ask for anything for herself.

Her hand rose to lightly skim his cheekbone and then his mouth and finally his jaw. "What's wrong? Tell me."

He wanted to. God, how he wanted to, because there were still things he didn't remember and things that weren't clear. Like the trip on the yacht with his friends. He wasn't even sure which friends had been there. Shouldn't he remember that? And he didn't remember the beach, and he didn't remember a fight, and he didn't remember going overboard.

If his memory had returned, why were those details still blank?

"I just want to remember the yacht," he said after a moment, hating the turmoil within him. He'd always known himself. He'd always been confident. No, he didn't like this new version of himself. "I want to remember my friends and the circumstances that brought me to you."

She rubbed the line of his jaw and then lightly dragged her fingernails across the stubble of his beard. "I do, too. And then when I know what happened, I will find your friends and give them a piece of my mind because how dare they treat you so shabbily! How dare—"

He stopped her words with a kiss, and as he kissed her he felt a shaft of pain through his chest. She was, without a doubt, the very best thing he'd ever known, and soon he'd break her heart. And just maybe break his, too.

Josephine woke with a start, a familiar sound puncturing her dreams. It was a boat.

Her father's motorboat. She flung back the covers and practically jumped out of bed, trying to absorb the fact that her father was home two days earlier than expected.

A strong muscular arm reached for her. "Where are you going?" he murmured sleepily.

"My father's home," she answered, heart hammering, trying to imagine her father's reaction if he walked into the cottage and found her in bed with a strange man. Her father was tolerant but it would have been too much for him. She dragged her hair into a ponytail. "You stay here. I'll go speak with him."

"I'll go with you."

He stood unashamed before her, tall, muscular, tanned, *naked*. Heat rushed through her, and her hands shook as she pulled on a sundress, covering her nudity, suddenly aware that she wasn't at all prepared for this moment. She'd convinced herself that her father would like him, but would he?

"Let me talk to him first, and then I'll bring him inside and introduce you two. I think it'd be better if I tell him what's happened—"

"Why are you upset? Will he be angry to find me here?"

"Not if you're dressed. But he's a father. I'm his little girl."

"Understood."

She pulled up the covers and then, glancing at the bed, realized how it would look. She took one of the pillows and a quilt and carried them to the living room, where she made a second bed on the ground.

He'd followed her into the living room, brow lifting quizzically. "My bed, I take it?"

"Yes." She shot him a desperate look. "Do you mind?"

"Am I really to sleep there?"

"If you'd prefer, *I* can sleep there—"

"Don't be foolish. I love sleeping on the floor."

"You don't mean that."

"True. But for you, I'd do anything." And then he pulled her into his arms and kissed her hard, the kiss hot and possessive. When he lifted his head, his blue gaze scorched her with its heat. "And I do mean that."

He released her and Josephine slipped out of

the cottage and ran down to the beach where her father was anchoring the boat. He was just reaching for the second line when he saw her. "Perfect timing," her father called.

She took the line from him and attached it to the mooring buried deep in the sand. He jumped out to give her a hand.

"You're back early," she said as he finished attaching the heavy chain through the iron loop.

"I was worried about you. I couldn't reach you on the radio."

"It broke a few days after you left."

"And you couldn't fix it?"

"I dropped it, smashing too many parts."

"I bought a new one, just in case."

"Smart thinking." She pushed her hair back from her face, feeling ridiculously nervous. She wasn't used to feeling this way, not around her father. "How was your trip? Everything go all right?"

"Everything went well. Had some good news while at the university. Picked up some more grant money, which is always nice."

"Money pays bills."

"Also necessary when restocking supplies." He waded back into the water and climbed into the boat and began dragging boxes and crates forward. "How have things been here? Anything exciting?"

She darted a glance toward the stone house. "Actually, yes. Far more exciting than usual." She took a quick breath. "We have a visitor."

Her dad stopped in his tracks, slowly straightening. "A what?"

"A visitor." She smiled brightly. "It's quite the story, too. You see, he went overboard and I saved him." She gulped more air, needing courage. "He was injured in the accident. He's lost his memory. Can't remember anything, not his name or where he's from."

"He's been alone with you this entire time?"

"Not the entire time. Just a week or so."

"A week or so." He paused, his weathered forehead creasing even more deeply. "Here? On the island?"

"Yes."

"Where is he now?"

"Inside the house. I asked him to stay there while I told you about him. I knew it'd be a shock. It was a shock to me—" she broke off as her dad jumped over the side of the boat and started for the house. "What are you doing?"

"Going to tell this fellow to pack up—"

"Pack what?" she cried, running to catch up with him. "He went overboard. He has nothing!"

"Great. It'll make it that much easier to ferry him to Antreas and hand him over to officials there."

"What are you talking about?"

"You know nothing about this man. He could be dangerous."

"If he was dangerous, wouldn't I know it by now?"

"I'll be the judge of that."

"Dad, stop. Listen." She grabbed his coat sleeve, tugged on it hard, stopping him. "He has *amnesia*."

"Which would make him all the more unpredictable. You're lucky he hasn't hurt you—"

"Why would I hurt her when she saved my life?" Alexander said, his deep voice catching them both by surprise. He approached her father and extended a hand. "I'm grateful for your daughter's bravery, Professor Robb."

Her father warily shook his hand. "I understand you've had an accident."

"I did."

Her father stepped back, still studying him, his expression shuttered. His closed expression worried her. Her father was a professor—his career had been filled with young people, students—and he was usually affable, friendly. He wasn't now. What was wrong?

"Let's get the supplies in," her father said, turning to her. "While you put away the food, I'll set up the radio."

"Can I help?" Alexander asked.

"No, but thank you," her father said.

"Then I'll give you some time to catch up."

In the cottage, Josephine kept glancing at her father as she unpacked the groceries and various supplies needed for life on Khronos. Her father worked on the radio, attaching it to the solar panels that would maintain a constant charge. Normally he'd talk to her while he worked. This morning he was silent.

She folded her arms and faced him. "You're upset."

"Do you know who he is?" he asked. "This ship-wrecked man of yours?"

"No. But he's obviously European, and wealthy. It was a huge yacht, incredibly luxurious."

Finished with the radio, her father went to his backpack and retrieved his computer and a pile of newspapers. "He's a prince from the kingdom of Aargau. And he's been missing for over a week."

She laughed. "A prince?"

Her father didn't smile. His expression was stony.

"A *prince*?" she repeated, her throat suddenly scratchy.

"Yes."

"You're sure?"

Her father flung down the stack of newspapers. "It's in all the news, in papers from all over the world. Everyone is looking for him. It's been in the headlines daily. At first he was merely missing, but they have now begun to worry he's not going to be found—at least not found alive. All the more tragic as he's supposed to be getting married in just a few weeks."

He was getting married?

No…

No.

"Maybe it's a different person. Maybe—" she broke off as her gaze fell on the top newspaper, the headline paired with a photo. The bold headline read "Prince Alexander Feared Dead," and while she didn't recognize the name, she recognized the face in the photo.

It *was* him.

And his name was Alexander.

Alexander. She said the name silently, rolling it over in her mind, before looking back down at the photo. Her mystery man, her beloved stranger, wasn't a rich Italian but a Mediterranean prince. Thirty-four-year-old Prince Alexander Julius Alberici, who was engaged to marry Princess Danielle Roulet at the end of this month.

Her father returned to the radio, adjusting the signal. "I'm going to call the Greek authorities," he said. "They'll in turn alert the authorities in Aargau. I imagine they'll send help right away, probably a helicopter."

She crossed the floor to the open window, where she stood facing the sea. She couldn't see Alexander, not from where she stood, but she knew he was out there, probably in the sheltered cove.

"Do you have to call today?" she asked quietly, her back to her father, her gaze still on the bay. "Can you wait until the morning? Give us this last day."

"That would be cruel. His family thinks he's dead."

She nodded, swallowing hard around the lump filling her throat. She didn't want to be cruel, but she would miss him. Terribly.

"Can you at least wait until I'm gone?" she asked, glancing over her shoulder to where her father sat at the table with the radio.

"I'm going to call soon," her father answered.

She fought the salty sting of tears and forced back the lump making it difficult to swallow.

It was ending so quickly. She'd thought she'd have at least two more days before her father returned, but instead he was here and taking control, and she was grateful he was doing the right thing, the proper thing, but she wasn't ready to say goodbye to Alexander.

She didn't want to be here when they came for him. She couldn't imagine parting, never mind surrounded by strangers who didn't understand what the past week had been like.

It had been heaven on earth.

She'd never been so happy in her entire life.

And yet he wasn't hers. He was never meant to be hers. What they'd shared here on Khronos was a mistake—no, she wouldn't call it that, but a fluke, something that hadn't been meant to be. And while the time they'd shared couldn't be taken from them, there was no future for them. It was unlikely their paths would ever cross again.

"I don't want to be here when they come for him," she said quietly, her gaze meeting her father's before shifting away. "May I have your permission to take the boat to Antreas? I haven't been off Khronos in ages. It'll be good for me to get out and do something."

"You don't want to see him off?"

"You know how I am about goodbyes. I find them painful."

"Won't the prince be offended?"

"It will be better for him if people don't know he was here alone with me. It will be better if help comes and they find you."

"The truth will get out. It always does."

"But that won't be my problem then. He'll be home in Aargau with his family and his fiancée." The words stuck in her throat. She managed a tight smile. "And at least this way I'll have some dignity. Goodbyes always hurt too much."

"You've been this way ever since you lost your mom—"

"I don't want to talk about her. Let me gather

a few things quickly as I'd like to leave soon. I'll take the boat to Antreas for the night and return by noon tomorrow."

"It's too far on your own."

"It's a straight shot north. I'll be fine, and I've done it before." She managed another small, brittle smile. "And when I return tomorrow, all will be well, and life will return to normal."

CHAPTER FIVE

ALEXANDER RETURNED FROM his swim to discover Josephine had left, and she'd gone without a word to him. She'd gone without a goodbye.

Her father attempted a weak explanation, which only made Alexander grit his teeth. It was a battle to hide his shock and disappointment.

"She didn't know how to say goodbye," Professor Robb added. "She doesn't like to cry."

"And why would she cry?" Alexander retorted stiffly.

The professor pushed a set of newspapers across the rough-hewn table, giving him a glimpse of headline after headline.

"Aargau's Prince Alex Missing"
"Tragedy on Yacht in Aegean Sea"
"Royal Prince Feared Dead"

"She knows who I am," Alexander said.

Professor Robb nodded. "But so do you, don't you?"

"I started remembering pieces a few days ago, but it wasn't until yesterday that I remembered my name and who I was."

"You didn't tell her."

Alexander didn't reply. "When will she return?"

"After you're gone."

"And when will that be?"

"I suspect help will be arriving later this afternoon."

The professor was right.

A helicopter from Aargau's Royal Navy arrived within hours, a medic on board in case Alexander needed care, but after a quick exam, he was cleared to fly, and they left Khronos.

Alexander didn't speak the entire flight to Aargau, nor did he speak as the Mercedes whisked him from the helipad to the palace. It was just a fifteen-minute drive and he stared out the window seeing, but not seeing, the streets of Roche, Aargau's capital city, home for the past one hundred sixty-five years to the royal Alberici family.

His family.

As the chauffeur drove him, with cars driven by security ahead and behind him, he wondered why he didn't feel relief that he was home.

He wondered why sights that were familiar didn't fill him with any comfort or pleasure.

Instead he felt only an oppressive sense of dread. He knew his father was ill—he remembered that clearly—but there was something missing in his memories, something that didn't explain the dread that felt like a lead weight in his gut.

Perhaps it was because he didn't remember

in his chair and Alexander went to his aid but his father brushed him away. "I'm not so frail that I can't sit up in my own chair."

"Never doubted your strength, sir."

His father cleared his throat and then coughed and coughed. And coughed some more. It was a long time before he could speak. "Your cousin," he rasped, eyes watering, voice quavering. "He's been quite anxious about your return. Damian's been checking in a half-dozen times a day."

"Hoping to inherit, I'm sure."

His father looked at him hard from beneath dark brows. "He has always respected the crown, unlike you."

"I was a boy when I said those things. Don't you think it's time to forgive?"

"I forgave you, but I won't forget."

Alexander held back the words he wanted to say. There was no point in defending himself, no point in arguing his case. It would change nothing. "I would have it no other way, Father."

"Princess Danielle's family has also been in touch daily. Have you spoken yet with her?" His mother asked, diverting the attention. "She's been frantic."

"Does she do *frantic*? I've only ever known her be the epitome of calm."

"Not frantic as in frenzied, but concerned," his mother conceded. "Which is why we like her so

his time on the yacht. Perhaps it was because he feared questions about the trip and his injury and his questionable memory. He didn't want to alarm his mother by letting her know that there were things he didn't remember. He needed to protect her from more stress. The past nine days couldn't have been easy for her.

Arriving at the palace, the gates opened for the parade of black Mercedes and then closed behind them. The palace was surrounded by thick walls dating back to the fifteenth century, and portions of that early fortress remained: a chapel, a tower, a prison dungeon. Newer buildings had risen around the medieval architecture, sometimes incorporating them, sometimes ignoring them. The Alberici family lived in the eighteenth-century palace, and guards and staff filled some of the other buildings. Years ago Alexander had claimed the tower as his own, converting each floor into rooms of his own. He had a private gym on the ground floor and an office one floor above that. His private library was on the third floor, with access to a guest suite on the fourth. The stairwell between the fourth and fifth floors led to the roof and the parapet where antique cannons remained.

When he needed to be home for long periods, he'd retreat to the tower guest suite, sleeping there to give himself some much-needed privacy. No one entered the tower without his permission, and he limited access when he was in residence to his own butler and valet.

His butler and valet were on the palace front steps as the motorcade drew to a stop, and they ushered him to his suite of rooms in the palace, where he showered, shaved and dressed.

"Are you well, Your Highness?" his valet asked after giving Alexander's coat a tug, adjusting the fit over his shoulders.

"Yes, thank you," Alexander answered.

"You have quite a cut on your head, sir."

"It's nothing."

"The doctor has seen you?"

"A navy doctor checked me out on the way here."

"Very good, sir."

And then Alexander was off, leaving his suite for that of his parents' rooms.

The meeting with his mother and father was brief. His father was in a chair, his eyes closed, when Alexander entered the room. His mother, Serena, was sitting in a chair nearby, embroidering. She'd taken up embroidery a few years ago and now it was rare to see her in private without a needle and thread in her hands.

Seeing that his father was sleeping, he paused at his mother's chair, stooping to kiss her forehead. At fifty-five she was slim and elegant and until recently had looked far younger than her years, but

his father's change of health had unfairly aged her. "Hello, Mother."

She reached up to pat his cheek and tears filled her eyes. "Alexander," she said, the quiver in her voice betraying the stress of the past few weeks.

He glanced to his father's chair. His father looked shockingly thin, his complexion gray. "How is he?"

Her shoulders shrugged. "He's—"

"Tired of worrying about you, you thankless scoundrel," his father answered, his voice hoarse and thin.

Alexander smiled faintly. His father wasn't joking, either. He'd been a disappointment to his father ever since he was a boy and had refused to hunt and shoot animals and whip his horse and do any number of things that a male should do to prove his dominance. "You can stop worrying then. I'm back, safe and sound," Alexander said lightly.

"It crossed my mind that you were deliberately staying away, enjoying our discomfort."

"No, never." He glanced down at his mother, his expression softening. "I'd never want to distress Mother. Now, you, you're a different matter." His lips were curved, his tone dry and slightly mocking because that was how he and his father communicated. With biting sarcasm and withering disdain.

"Ha, I knew it." His father struggled to

much. She won't embarrass you. She won't embarrass us."

"A perfect wife," he murmured.

And yet his mother heard, her dark blond eyebrows rising. "I thought you liked her."

"And I do," Alexander answered. "She's a perfectly lovely princess."

"Faultless," Serena added.

"Right." He gave her a slight bow and then another in the direction of his father, and he was off. The great homecoming was over.

Alexander's close friends were warmer in their greetings. They descended on him, gathering in his large suite in Alberici Palace, exclaiming over his tan, offering fierce hugs and pats on the back. These were men who'd grown up with him and gone to university with him and served in the Royal Navy with him, and they were damn glad to see him home.

"We were desperate," Gerard said as they all took seats in Alexander's living room. "Once we discovered you were gone, we notified the palace immediately, and they sent planes and helicopters, and the Greek Air Force and Navy joined in the search, but there was no sign of you. We honestly feared the worst."

"When did you realize I was missing?" Alexander asked, the only one not to sit.

Gerard grimaced. "When you didn't come out

for breakfast, and then lunch, I knew something was wrong. I ended up breaking your door down."

"Well, I broke it down," Rocco corrected. "Gerard was trying but not very successfully."

Everyone laughed, but the laughter died to an uncomfortable silence.

"Have you talked to her yet?" Marc asked after a moment. "She's been really upset."

"Danielle?"

"No, Claudia," Marc answered. "I hate playing the big-brother card, but it seems that you owe her an apology."

"Not now," Gerard murmured. "He's only just returned. This isn't the time."

"Why not now?" Marc retorted. "Better to handle this now without Damian here, don't you think?"

Alexander glanced from Marc to Gerard to Rocco. There were undercurrents he couldn't read. Things had happened that he didn't understand. He still had no memory of the trip and yet clearly he needed his memories. "What is this about Damian? And where is he?"

His three friends all glanced at each other before Gerard, the diplomat, answered. "It's been a difficult ten days for him. You and he had that… falling-out…on the ship. And then you went missing. He's been juggling shock and grief—"

"About what?" Alexander interrupted, frustration sharpening his voice.

"Damian said you'd consumed more liquor than we knew. Maybe it was true," Rocco said bluntly.

"And not to play big brother again, but Claudia wasn't yours anymore, Alberici," Marc added. "You broke up with her, not the other way around. You should have left her alone."

The gathering abruptly ended. Alexander asked Gerard to remain behind. He and Gerard had been roommates at the Naval Academy and then had served together all three years in the Royal Navy, and there was no one Alexander trusted more. Gerard was a vault. The man knew how to serve, protect, and keep a secret.

"I need you to tell me what you remember of that last night," Alexander said after the other two had gone.

"What's happened?" Gerard asked quietly. "Something has, hasn't it?"

"Other than the fact that I'm being accused of hitting on my ex-girlfriend and fueling a feud with my cousin?"

"None of that took place?"

"I don't believe so."

"But you don't know."

"I'd like to look at the footage from the yacht's security camera."

"I already requested it."

"And?"

"There is none."

"What?"

"There is no footage, that end of the ship was never equipped with security cameras."

Unbelievable. Alexander closed his eyes and held his breath, containing his disappointment. He'd been counting on footage helping him piece together the mystery of what happened on the boat, and why.

"So what do you remember of that last night?" Alexander said, when he could trust himself to speak calmly.

"You were having a drink with us and said you'd be right back, but you never returned."

"What time did I excuse myself?"

"It was after dinner, so maybe ten. Annaliese said it might have been a little earlier. Gigi thought it was a bit later. But ten is a safe bet." Gerard watched Alexander pace the length of the room and the tense silence stretched. After several minutes passed, he said, "You're worrying me, Alex. You are the most detail-oriented person I know. Nothing escapes your attention. Why all the questions? What's happened?"

"I don't know," Alexander said simply, facing his friend. "I've told no one this, but I trust you, and I need your help. I have no memory of that night at all. It's all a blank, and I was hoping you could help me clear up some of the mystery."

Gerard's jaw dropped. "So you don't know how you ended up in the water?"

"I don't remember anything from the trip." He hesitated. "But it's worse than that. For an entire week, I had no memory at all. For a week I didn't know who I was. I didn't know my name."

"How did you manage?"

"I was rescued by a girl on an island. She saved my life and took care of me."

"That's a story."

"It was like a story," he agreed. "The Prince and the Mermaid."

"There is a story like that by Hans Christian Andersen."

"Does it end happily?"

"For the prince."

"And the mermaid?"

"She sacrifices herself for him and turns to sea foam."

"I don't think I'd like that story."

Gerard's brow creased. "I'm worried about you, Alex. If Damian knew this, it could be quite bad for you."

"I know." Alexander sighed and dragged a hand through his hair. "I need the missing pieces. I need my memory. And I definitely need the security footage from the yacht."

* * *

Josephine was sure that once she returned to Khronos, life would be fine. Prince Alexander would be gone and she'd be able to focus on her work again.

She expected some sadness and knew she'd miss his company, but she'd lost her mother and lived, and so she'd survive Alexander's departure just fine. The tears she cried at night into her pillow were just part of the process of letting him go. And she would let him go. The intense memories would eventually fade, and over time she'd think of him less and less until one day she could remember him with something other than pain.

It was a good plan, and it might have worked out that way if she hadn't discovered she was pregnant two weeks after his departure for Aargau.

Josephine had suspected within days of Alexander leaving Khronos that she *could* be pregnant, but she'd told herself she was being dramatic, letting her imagination run away with her, which was why she waited almost two weeks to take an over-the-counter pregnancy test that she bought in Athens when she was there with her father for a foundation meeting.

She'd waited until she was alone to buy the test, and then in her hotel room she followed the steps and told herself everything would be fine, that she didn't need to panic or worry—

And then came the immediate positive result.

She *was* pregnant.

And Josephine sat on the side of the bathtub, holding the stick, thinking that she'd known. She'd known because her body felt different. Her breasts were fuller and more sensitive, and she felt nauseous and fatigued.

She couldn't even pretend to be shocked. They'd made love a half-dozen times and they hadn't taken precautions. Yes, he'd withdrawn, but it wasn't true birth control. It was far from foolproof. She didn't know why they hadn't discussed it more. She didn't know why it hadn't been a more urgent issue. It was stupid. She'd behaved irrationally. She'd behaved as if she was the one with amnesia, not he.

And she wasn't just pregnant, but pregnant with the child of one of the most fascinating, wealthy royal families in the world.

Josephine felt sick. Heartsick. Disgusted with herself, disgusted by her lapse in judgment.

If she went to her father she knew what he would say. He would say she had three options: terminate the pregnancy and tell no one, keep the child and tell no one, or keep the child but tell Alexander because he had a right to know.

It took little or no thought to eliminate option one: she wasn't going to end the pregnancy. That wasn't an option, not for her. She tried to imagine raising Alexander's child in secret, and that wasn't a viable option, either. It wasn't right or fair, not to him or their child. But how could she just show up at the Alberici palace in Roche and demand an audience? Never mind just a week before Alexander's wedding to Princess Danielle?

Stomach churning, she waited for her father to return from his meeting. "I need to reach Prince Alexander," she told him. "I need to speak with him about a matter of some…urgency."

Her father eyed her in silence for a long minute. "You're pregnant, aren't you?"

She nodded.

"Well, that explains the food poisoning. It wasn't food poisoning at all."

"I had hoped."

"So had I." He sighed and shook his head. "This is going to change your life. It will never be the same."

"You don't think I'll be a good mother?"

"It's not that simple. I'm not a monarchist, and I don't know all the laws in Aargau, but this isn't just any baby. You're carrying the future king's heir."

"Maybe I shouldn't tell him."

"You are as honest as they come, Josephine. You'd never keep the truth from him, or a child from his father. You wouldn't be able to live with yourself. So contact the palace security—I have a number, they left it with me when they came for him—but don't expect this meeting of yours to be easy. Your news could change everything."

The return to Khronos was so different from his departure two and a half weeks earlier. When he left, he hadn't thought he'd see Josephine again and he'd been livid with her, seething the entire trip to Roche. At the time, he didn't know what had upset him more—the fact that she'd left Khronos without telling him, or that she'd left the island without him telling her who he was.

He'd known that day, and every day since, that he should have told her his memory had returned. He'd been painfully aware that he should have handled things differently.

And now he was to see her again. She'd sent word through his security that there was an urgent private matter, and she'd asked his security how she should best deliver this urgent, sensitive information.

He'd known at once why she was reaching out. It was the only reason she would reach out.

Alexander requested the helicopter and flight crew for the following morning and now they were traveling above the blue-green water. Soon they'd be touching down on Khronos. He wondered if she had any idea he was on his way or that if her news was as he expected, then he'd be taking her back to Aargau with him. Today.

* * *

Helicopters were impossibly noisy, their turning blades impossibly distinctive. Josephine emerged from the small house, her pen still in her hand as she shielded her eyes to look up into the sky. The huge helicopter was flying low and coming directly toward her.

Her heart fell even as her stomach lurched, not a good combination when she was already nauseous.

Her father stepped out from the house, as well. His brow creased as he took in the helicopter dropping even lower. "He must have gotten your message," her father said.

She swallowed hard, her legs suddenly weak. "Maybe it's someone else."

"It's the same helicopter that came before. If he is any man at all, he'll be inside it and eager to speak with you."

Josephine wanted to throw up. She put a hand to her middle to slow the churning sensation that made her feel so sick. "You sound pleased."

"I'll be pleased if he comes in person to sort this out with you." He glanced at her, his expression suddenly critical. "Perhaps you'd like to change and comb your hair."

"Why? Because he's a prince?"

"No, because he's the man you love."

Josephine refused to change out of her yellow checked sundress, but she did run a brush through her hair and then pulled it back into a smooth ponytail, and then she took a seat at the table in the house and waited.

It wasn't long before she heard his footsteps outside and then his rap on the door that was already open.

She rose, hating how nervous she felt. "*Prince* Alexander Alberici," she said, accenting the word *Prince*. It wasn't polite, but then, she didn't feel polite. How could she when she was suddenly blisteringly angry?

"May I come in?" he said formally, still standing on her threshold.

"You know the house. You know your way around."

He entered, stooping slightly to clear the low doorway and then straightening once he was inside. His gaze swept the stone walls and rugged beams running across the ceiling. "Nothing's changed," he said.

"It's been this way for a hundred years. I expect it'll remain this way for another hundred."

He crossed the floor, glancing right and then left. "Your father?"

"Is at his desk in the foundation office." She struggled to contain her temper. "So no, there is no one here. It's just you and me. We won't be overheard."

"I wasn't worried about that. I wanted to be polite and pay my respects."

"How kind of you."

"You are angry."

"I am." She hadn't even realized just how deeply upset she was until he stepped through her door looking even more handsome than she remembered. He'd been beautiful to her in her father's faded chambray work shirts and linen shorts, but now in elegant trousers, dark shirt, and dark tailored blazer, he looked powerful. Magnetic. He was a man of position and wealth. And he knew it, too.

"You didn't have to reach out to me," he said, slowly walking around the central room, studying everything as if he'd never seen it before.

She hated his slow, lazy perusal because she was sure it wasn't lazy at all. He was doing his best to remember details. Or perhaps he was checking details against his memory. Either way, he had no right to be so relaxed, so indolent, in her home.

Her arms crossed over her chest, fingers curling into small, tight fists. "Does Princess Danielle know you're here?"

"We're not married yet."

"What does that even mean?"

"She doesn't get access to my personal schedule."

"Does she even know about me?"

"The palace hasn't released any information about you." He gave her a considering glance. "Unless you'd like the palace to release information?"

She shot him a furious look, giving him the full measure of her wrath. "When did your memory return?" She asked, her voice flat, hard. "At what point on Khronos did you know who you were?"

"The day before your father returned."

She stared at him, clearly struggling. "You should have told me."

"Yes."

"Why didn't you?"

"Because at that point I wasn't ready to lose you."

Her mouth tightened; her jaws ground together. She was not going to cry. She would not allow herself to show any weakness or emotion at all. "You mean you weren't ready to stop having sex."

His black eyebrow lifted. "Is that what we were doing? Having sex?"

"Unprotected sex. And there were…are…consequences."

"I suspected that was why you reached out to the palace."

"You're not shocked?"

"As you said, there are consequences."

"You sound so cavalier," she gritted out. "You must have a plan in mind. A suggestion for managing this *complication*."

"Are you enjoying yourself?"

"No. I'm sick and heartsick and I should have

heard the truth from you. I should have heard the truth, if you knew it."

"Agreed. I was wrong. I am truly sorry."

His apology caught her off guard and she felt herself sag, so she sat down in the chair at the table, her hands balling in her lap.

He crossed the floor, approaching her, so tall that she had to tip her head back to look him in the eye.

"I didn't tell you," he added, "because I was determined to find a way to save us."

"Save us?" She made a soft, hoarse sound of protest. "How? You were engaged to someone else. Your wedding was weeks away. You weren't free to be with me. You weren't free to make love to me."

He crouched in front of her, his hands on her knees. "I can't change what happened when I didn't have my memory—"

"No, but that doesn't mean I don't regret it." She pushed his hands off her knees, feeling burned. "All of it."

"No."

"*Yes.* I hate that week we spent together. I hate that I fe—" She broke off, swallowing hard, smashing the words that had nearly escaped her lips. *I fell in love with you.* But she couldn't love him. Not anymore. She'd smash her feelings now, just as she'd suppressed the words. What had happened was history. The past was behind them. The only thing to do now was move forward without him. Somehow.

"Have you seen a doctor?" he asked.

She shook her head.

"Then how do you know?"

"I took a test in Athens yesterday, and I took it because I've never been late, and my body is different. Everything feels different. I'm violently ill, sometimes in the morning, sometimes at night. The only time I seem to be okay is in the afternoon and early evening." She fell silent for a moment before drawing a breath for courage. "I wouldn't have reached out to you if I wasn't certain. I am pregnant. And I intend to keep the baby. I don't need anything from you—"

"Of course you do. It's my child, too."

"I'm not asking for support. I'm not asking for—"

"Anything, yes, I know. But it doesn't work that way, *cara*. You are carrying my child, my heir. You might not ask for anything, but that doesn't mean you don't get everything."

She blinked, not understanding. "I'm sorry. I don't follow. What is everything?"

"Marriage. My home. My kingdom."

"But I don't want any of those—"

"I knew you'd say that. I was actually counting on you saying that. You didn't sleep with me to become pregnant. You didn't make love to me for any ulterior motive. You are not one of those women that try to entrap a man."

"Maybe it's time for you to go. You know the truth. I've kept nothing from you—"

"We need you to see a doctor. We need to be sure."

"I am sure."

"Yes, but I can't end my engagement to Danielle without proof. It wouldn't be fair to her."

"I don't want you to end your engagement to her. You're engaged to her. You must marry her—"

"I can't, not if you're carrying my child."

Her lips parted but no sound came out.

"The babe you're carrying is Aargau's future king or queen." Alexander rose. "I shall go look for your father and let him know you'll be returning to Roche with me."

He was so very different from her Alexander. But then, on the other hand, he wasn't. He'd always been rather imperious, if not downright commanding. She'd known from the moment he'd first spoken to her that he was a man familiar with authority and accustomed to being obeyed. But that didn't mean she had to fall in with his plans. She'd fallen in love with a man, not a prince, and she wanted the man, not the prince. "No, I'm not going."

His mouth tightened. Creases fanned from his

eyes. He looked as if he was hanging on to his patience by a thread. "I'll explain to your father—"

"No need to look for me, I'm here." Her father stepped through the doorway. "I've heard most of what's been said. And I agree with Prince Alexander. You should see a doctor. You should be certain. Feelings are not facts, and what you both need now are facts. Having clear facts will help you make the right decisions."

CHAPTER SIX

SUNLIGHT PIERCED THE TALL, narrow windows of the tower suite. Holding her breath, Josephine watched the light pattern the smooth stone floor, focusing on where the blue-gray fieldstone disappeared beneath the pale ivory-knotted fringe of the burgundy and peach antique carpet.

If she stayed very still and very calm, she could lose herself in the streaks of golden light.

If she stayed very still and very calm, she could almost believe she hadn't been locked for days in a high tower without any connection to the outside world.

And then, since she *was* pretending, she could pretend her room, with its high vaulted ceiling, lovely, narrow leaded windows, and imposing four-poster bed in the middle of the floor, was a luxurious historic hotel room, and she was a guest at this stunning five-hundred-year-old castle, making her much envied by those who loved luxury travel. She would also pretend that the man who'd locked her here, the man she'd fallen in love with, was a handsome, kind prince instead of a cold, heartless one.

Unfortunately, Josephine wasn't good at sustaining the pretend game. It wasn't that she didn't have an imagination, but being the daughter of two scientists, she was more practical than impractical and loathed everything about her tower, and the man who'd locked her here.

Jo sat up straighter as she heard the scrape of the key turning in the lock. She fought a momentary panic because once the door opened, she couldn't play her games of pretend. It was so much harder to manage her emotions with Alexander in the room.

Four weeks ago Josephine wouldn't have believed any of this was possible. But then, four weeks ago she hadn't known who Alexander was.

Four weeks ago, neither had he.

Now she wished she'd never told him she was pregnant. She'd thought she was doing the right thing, the honest and fair thing. But Josephine regretted her decisions with her whole heart as Alexander was neither honest nor fair, as it was his decision to put her here in this tower suite. It was his decision to lock the door. It was his decision to cut her off from communication with the world, but locking her away wouldn't help his cause. If he imagined that a few days of solitary confinement would weaken her resolve, he was painfully mistaken. She'd spent weeks, *months*, alone on Khronos while her father was off teaching. She wasn't afraid to be alone, and she wasn't easily intimidated.

But she was beginning to realize that her upbringing, so isolated from society, had not prepared her for dealing with complex relationships, and she suddenly doubted herself. She'd always thought she was a good judge of character, but apparently she wasn't. It seemed that she knew too much about science and too little about human beings. Which was why she'd told Alexander on arriving in Aargau that she'd include him in their child's life, even share parental responsibilities with him—because that was the fair thing to do—but he'd refused to even consider co-parenting. Their baby would live with him in the palace. Their baby required both mother and father, and they'd do it together. Married. And that would never ever happen. She'd never agree to marrying him, not after he'd revealed his true colors.

The door swung open and Prince Alexander Julius Alberici stood on the threshold, tall, broad shouldered, and impeccably groomed. His thick black hair was ruthlessly combed back, hiding the fact that it had an inclination to curl. His blue eyes focused on her with that laser focus that always made her feel as if he could see straight through her.

She sat up taller, her own shoulders squaring, chin lifting defiantly. She'd been told on first arriving in Roche that she should curtsy before him, and she'd laughed. *Laughed.* "I'd sooner have a lobotomy," she'd snapped.

Prince Alexander had heard and his lips had tightened.

His mouth—which she'd once thought so lovely—tightened now, but she no longer cared. Right now she didn't care what he thought, and right now she didn't care what he did, as long as he let her return to Khronos. It felt as if every good and tender feeling had been smashed, and it was his fault. He'd done this to her. To *them*.

"Can I help you?" she asked coolly.

Alexander entered the tower bedroom, unsurprised to find her where he'd last seen her, in the middle of her bed with a pile of books around her, her expression hard and shuttered. Her sketchbook was open next to her, a charcoal pencil against white paper, but the page was blank.

"How are you this morning?" he asked, stepping into the room, the door closing and locking behind him.

He saw her head turn, her honey hair scraped back from her face, pulled into a severe knot at her nape. Her green gaze focused on the door, her lips compressing with displeasure as the lock scraped closed. He knew she hated being locked in, and he hated locking her in. But he wasn't about to run the risk of her leaving Aargau in the dark of night, not when she was pregnant with his child.

"I am as tired of this as you," he said flatly, approaching the bed. "I just want a resolution. I want us to move forward."

Her head jerked up, eyes flashing with contempt. Even with her hair drawn back and not a bit of makeup to enhance her features, she was strikingly beautiful. He'd wondered when he first returned from Greece if he'd imagined her and her breathtaking beauty. He hadn't. If anything, she was more ethereal, and even lovelier than he'd remembered.

But her delicate beauty belied her strength. Josephine was livid, and she was not about to be strong-armed into marriage. "I don't like this any more than you," he added. "Marry me so we can be done with this. We were friends once—"

"*Not* friends."

"On Khronos you told me you loved me, Josephine. You said the words."

Color flooded her cheeks, making her eyes brighter. "I had no idea you weren't free. I had no idea you were...*you*."

"Neither did I."

"For your information, I liked the other you better, the one with amnesia. The one that didn't know his name, because at least he knew how to be kind. What you're doing now is unforgivable. You can't lock women in towers. It's medieval. Machiavellian." Her chin lifted, her gaze locking with his. "Even *you* must know that it's not done."

"I'm not happy about this, *bella*. I would prefer you to have a normal guest suite. I would prefer to be able to introduce you to my family and friends—"

"And your fiancée, Princess Danielle Roulet? What about her? Or have you not given her any thought or consideration?"

"You know I ended my engagement to her the moment we had confirmation of your pregnancy." He leaned against one of the enormous wooden posters on the antique bed. "There is nothing standing in the way of our marriage now."

"Nothing but my objections, but apparently that doesn't signify in your world. You're a prince, and I'm just an ordinary American girl."

"Who will one day be queen."

"I don't want to be queen. I'm not marrying you."

"Josephine, I'm trying to make this work—"

"Locking me in a tower is not making it work, Alexander!"

"You shouldn't have tried to run away."

"I wasn't running away. I was simply leaving the castle."

"With the intention to take a ferry to Italy and then disappear into Europe." He gave her a sympathetic look. "Next time, don't admit so much to a taxi driver, especially when he's a member of palace security."

"I did think it strange that you had a taxi just waiting outside."

"He wasn't there for you, if that's any consolation."

"It's not."

"Can we agree that you're not going to run away anymore? Because if you can give me your word—"

"I'm not sure I can, Alexander. I'm sorry."

"I am, too, because the baby you carry is my heir and thus the heir to the Aargau throne, which gives you two choices—marry me, or grant me sole custody of our child."

He saw her lips press and pain shadow her eyes. "You know I'd never give up my child. You're not giving me a choice."

"Most women would jump at the opportunity to become Aargau's queen."

"I'm not one of them."

"You're offended because it's not a romantic proposal."

"I'm offended because you're arrogant and rude, and baffled by what you call a proposal. You've flung the word *marriage* at me as if I'm a dog being dangled a bone. But the bone, Your Highness, isn't remotely appealing."

Alexander was torn between amusement and outrage. He wondered what his old self would have thought of her response. He'd been told by his friends that his old self lacked a sense of humor. That was interesting because sometimes Josephine made him want to laugh. Or shake her. Or make fierce, hot love to her.

"I'm phrasing things badly," he said. "But we have a wedding to plan, *cara*. We can't keep arguing and wasting time. We have to marry soon. It's essential we avoid scandal."

"You mean it's essential to *you*. I don't care about the scandal."

"That's because you live on an uninhabited rock, apart from society. The rest of us, I'm afraid, are not so lucky."

"You're not serious."

"About the marriage, or being determined to avoid scandal?"

"Both."

"We don't do scandals in Aargau. There has never been a divorce in the Alberici family."

"Just unhappily married, is that it?"

"My parents and grandparents and great-grandparents all knew better then to air dirty laundry. If there is strife, it's dealt with privately, behind closed doors. As we are doing now."

"So women are routinely locked in chambers and towers here?"

"You failed to mention the dungeons."

"I suppose if you have a historic castle, one should use all the rooms."

His lips twisted faintly. She amused him, and yet their current situation was anything but laughable. The palace was in an uproar. His father wasn't speaking to him. His mother was quietly frantic. The public couldn't understand what had happened to their prince.

"I want out of this room," Josephine said clearly, firmly.

"And I want you out of this room. I'd like it to become my retreat again. It used to be one of my favorite rooms, but holding you hostage here has diminished my pleasure in it."

"Poor Prince Alexander. How you suffer!"

He had to smash the laughter. "You are in such a foul mood. Perhaps I should kiss you—"

"No!" She scooted back on the bed. "You come near me and I'll throw every book I have at your head. And I've a good arm. Believe me."

"I do. That's why I want to move forward. It's why I want to introduce you to my kingdom and my people, but I can't do that until we've come to an understanding."

"We can raise our child together without being married." She paused, her winged eyebrows arching even higher. "Or resorting to locking me away as if I'm a dangerous criminal. You must know your strong-arm tactics only make me dislike you and mistrust you more."

"Trust goes both ways."

"Absolutely, and when have I ever let you down? Or betrayed you in any way?"

"You left me on Khronos. You disappeared without a word. And then you tried to run away from here after we saw the doctor. Josephine, I accept that I haven't been the model prince, but you have a poor track record when it comes to staying in place."

"Fine. Next time I'll put up a few signs to advertise that I'm leaving so there won't be any mixed signals," she flashed, hiding how much he continued to hurt her. She told herself she didn't care about him anymore, but if that was true, why did his every word wound? Why did he have such power over her? Worse, how could this be the man she'd loved so passionately on Khronos? He was nothing but cold and hard and calculating. How had she not seen his true nature before?

"Give me your word that you will not run, and I'll move you from the tower to a proper suite in the palace. Better yet, accept my proposal and let us plan the wedding together so that our baby will be born without any shame or scandal surrounding his or her birth."

If only it were that easy, she thought, drawing her knees to her chest and wrapping her arms around her legs, trying to anchor herself, craving safety and stability. Ever since she'd arrived in Roche, she'd felt rootless. Lost. She desperately missed her life on Khronos, needing her work to give her days structure and purpose. "I want to return to Khronos," she whispered. "I want to go home."

"Not until after the baby is born, but then yes, you could go for a visit."

"A visit," she said, her voice trembling.

He said nothing and she glanced around the room, taking in the thick stone walls, the narrow windows, the heavy beamed ceiling. "You're punishing me."

"That's not fair."

"I was a virgin when I met you and now I'm pregnant. Doesn't seem fair at all."

"You wanted to be with me."

"Because I thought you were free. I thought you cared about me."

"I do care about you, which is why I'm marrying *you*, not Danielle."

"You're only marrying me because I'm pregnant!"

"Do you want me to deny it? No, it's true. I'm marrying you because you're carrying my child, but that doesn't invalidate my offer—"

"Oh, it does. It most certainly does, *Your Highness.*"

He sighed. "You're being childish."

"You're being hideous."

"We can't go back, Josephine. We can only go forward."

"And we will," she agreed huskily, "but not together. We might have created a baby together, but that doesn't mean we must punish ourselves for eternity—"

"Marriage is not hell."

"So says the man who had a girlfriend *and* a fiancée."

"I broke up with my girlfriend months before my engagement was announced."

"But you were privately engaged to the princess, weren't you?"

"We've had an understanding for years, yes, but Danielle also dated. She had relationships—"

"That still changes nothing. I'm not about to have my heart broken by a man who only cares for himself."

"But why would it be broken if you don't care for me? This isn't a love marriage, Josephine. It's a business deal, an arrangement to protect our child, who will inherit the Alberici wealth and title."

She blinked, hard. "So I don't matter."

His sigh was deep, heavy. "Of course you matter."

Her head dipped, her gaze dropped. "Please leave."

"It's time to put our child first. Stop with the selfishness—"

"*Me?* Selfish? Clearly, you don't remember Khronos or what happened there. But I do. And I was never selfish, never unkind, not toward you."

He left her then, and as the door closed behind him, she put her head down on her knees and fought tears.

She was exhausted and nauseous and sick of emotion. She wasn't used to feeling this much, and certainly not used to so little physical activity. For a girl who'd grown up outside, so close to nature that she felt she was an extension of the mountains and sea, being cooped up in a tower, in a castle, in a city, was a terrible punishment indeed.

Alexander descended the tower staircase to his office on the second floor, aware that Josephine wasn't wrong. He was different here. He had to be different here. On Khronos he'd been just a man. In Aargau he was the future king. He'd rather enjoyed being just a man. There had been freedom, and an ease he didn't know in his world here.

Aimee, his secretary, was at her desk when he entered the room and she glanced up at him, a troubled crease between her brows. "Her Highness has requested you join her in her rooms immediately." Aimee glanced at her watch. "That was nearly an hour ago. Her staff has followed up with me twice since, worried I haven't passed on the message."

"You knew where I was."

She gave a faint smile. "Yes, but you said not to bother you, and so I didn't."

Alexander crossed the Alberici castle grounds,

heading for the pale yellow eighteenth-century palace that travel guidebooks always falsely claimed had been inspired by the architecture of Versailles but in reality drew its inspiration from the Royal Palace at Caserta, which was just fifty years older and much closer geographically.

Alexander climbed the grand pink and yellow marble staircase to the second floor and headed back down the long corridor to the set of rooms that were his mother's. There was no need for him to knock as her butler opened the door, announcing him.

Queen Serena waved him to a chair near hers. "You kept me waiting long enough," she said as he sat down and stretched out his legs.

"I came to you the moment I was free."

"I'm hearing things, worrying things." She gave him a long look. "Do you have any news for me? News that would ease some of my anxiety, because your father grows weaker. He slept most of today. We're running short on time, particularly if you hope to have him present at your wedding. Or perhaps you intend to marry after he's gone?" His mother's tone was cool and distant. But then, it was the tone he knew best. She was beautiful and regal, elegant and refined, always cognizant of her power and responsibility as the queen of Aargau.

"Of course I want him there."

"Then the wedding needs to be sooner, not later."

"I understand."

"Then what is the problem, Alexander?"

"Josephine isn't…ready…to marry."

"Excuse me? She's carrying your child, the heir to the kingdom."

"I understand."

"The longer you wait, the more difficult it becomes from a PR standpoint. You understand that, don't you? We're trying to do damage control, Alexander, and all we need is a small, private service in the palace chapel—"

"Unless she wants the formal service in the cathedral."

"We don't have time to plan a formal wedding, and she doesn't need a big, formal wedding. Your father is very unhappy that she's trapped you."

"*I* trapped *her*, not the other way around."

"You're a prince. She is no one."

He knew his mother well enough to know that she wasn't trying to be cruel or rude, just honest. "She didn't care that I was a prince, and she is most definitely someone."

The queen sat back in her chair, her jaw dropping slightly. "You *love* her."

"I want her, yes. But love? I don't know about that. I was once teased for being so emotional. Now I'm criticized for not having feelings. Having feelings would make all of this easier."

"I didn't have…feelings when I married your

father. But they developed over time. Yours will develop, too." Her head tilted. She studied him intently. "Are you completely recovered from your accident?"

"Why do you ask?"

"You haven't been the same since you returned home. You are less...you."

He gave her a half bow. "Apologies. I shall try to be more...me."

"I don't appreciate the sarcasm, Alexander. It's very tense here, not simply because your father slips away from us a little more every day, but King Marcel Roulet is livid that his daughter has been profoundly embarrassed just a week before her wedding. And I've just been informed that you are keeping your American locked in your tower—"

"I did lock her in the first night. But she hasn't been locked in since."

"But she believes she's locked in."

He shrugged. "She has a tendency to run away. I need her to remain."

Her eyebrow lifted. "This is not how we conduct our affairs, nor is this how an Alberici royal handles his fiancée. Less drama, more efficiency, please. Put the ring on her finger. Give me a wedding date. We'll have a party this weekend—"

"Too soon."

"She could be *showing* by the next, Alexander."

"Then make it a week from now."

"An engagement party on a Wednesday?"

"Or Tuesday. We'll keep it small and intimate, for our closest friends and family only."

"Fine. But we'll need a portrait of the two of you to give the media." Her glance narrowed. "I don't suppose we can take your official engagement portrait and photoshop Danielle out and put your new girl in her place?"

"Was that a joke, Mother?"

Her lips curved faintly. "I was not always Queen Serena, Alexander. I, too, was once a young girl with a sense of humor and a hunger for adventure."

Josephine crossed to the window of her tower room, stepping up on the footstool she'd positioned beneath it, needing the extra height to look out the leaded glass. It was late afternoon, but due to the summer solstice a week ago, the sun was still high in the sky, shining brightly on the thick, gray slate roofs of the various castle buildings and then, farther out, the high, majestic stone walls that surrounded the castle itself.

She rested her chin on her fist, staring out, taking in Roche, Aargau's capital city famous for its medieval architecture and charming, narrow cobbled streets. She might have liked Roche, but after days of confinement she felt suffocated by all the walls and slate and cobbled stone. Her jaw tensed as her gaze went to the glimpse of sea beyond the city streets, the dark blue water calling to her, reminding her of Khronos.

A scrape sounded at the door, and the lock turned. She nearly fell off the stool as the door swung open and she took a sudden step back, misjudging the distance to the floor and needing to grab the wall to keep from falling down.

"Careful," a crisp, low feminine voice said from the doorway. "That's a good way to hurt yourself."

Josephine stiffened, surprised that it wasn't Alexander as he was the only one who'd been to visit her since she arrived, and yet she knew immediately who had come, having seen photos of her in magazines. "Queen Serena," she said faintly, letting go of the wall.

The slender blonde queen approached. "I haven't thwarted your escape plans, have I?"

Josephine thought she heard a hint of amusement in the older woman's voice. "I don't have Rapunzel's hair," she answered. "And even if I did, the window is a little narrow."

Serena stopped before her, her back straight, her bearing regal. In her icy-blue dress with the ropes of pearls, she looked every inch a queen. "I'm sorry I haven't been to see you sooner. I'm afraid our hospitality isn't what it should be."

"Does your son routinely lock his women up?"

"No, you're the first." She grimaced. "I'd like to say that it's a sign of his affection but you and I both know his behavior is inexcusable. One doesn't lock up beautiful young women in towers anymore. It's positively medieval."

"That's what I told him."

"Machiavellian."

"I said the very same thing."

"What are you going to do?"

"I don't know."

"What do you want to do?"

"Leave."

"What is keeping you here then?"

"Besides the locked door? The need to protect the baby." Josephine's chin lifted. "And not because he or she is an heir, but because he or she is my child."

"And Alexander's."

"I don't want Alexander, though. I realize he's your son, and you love him—"

"He's a man. Men are notoriously thickheaded and thin-skinned, but they have their uses and virtues."

Josephine wasn't sure how to take that last bit. She felt her shoulders tense, and she clasped her hands tightly. "I used to care for him very much, before he was—" she glanced around the room, and her hand followed in a sweeping gesture "—this."

"He's afraid of losing you."

"No, he's afraid of losing his heir, not me."

"If you truly believe that, you don't know my son."

Josephine's lips compressed and she held her tongue, not wanting to argue with the queen, because of course she'd take Alexander's side. She was his mother.

"But he won't lose his heir," Serena added after a moment. "You're not a woman who'd keep a child from his father, so there is something else driving him and making him act like a Neanderthal. Men usually only resort to caveman tactics when cornered and desperate." She glanced from Josephine to the bed, still piled high with books. "You're a scientist. Don't let your emotions cloud your brain. I understand you have a very good brain, so use it. Put my son on notice. Make him earn your favor."

"That will never happen."

"Fine. Then make him earn your trust, but do *something* so that you feel properly empowered and can respect yourself, if not him."

Josephine frowned. "You don't think I respect myself?"

"I think you know what you need to do, but your pride is keeping you from making the right decisions."

"Your solution is for me to marry Alexander."

"I have no solutions, but I do have a preference, and that is for my grandchild to grow up in a stable, loving home."

Josephine looked at the queen for a long, tense moment. "What happens now? When you leave, do you just lock me back in?"

"No. I have no patience for locked doors, secrets, or games."

"So I could leave now with you if I wanted."

Serena's fair head tipped. "Is that what you truly want? To leave here now?"

"I want Alexander to stop intimidating me."

"Then isn't it time to stand your ground?"

The queen walked out, and true to her word, after she left the door remained open, wide-open. Josephine waited a minute, and then another, and another, wondering when one of the palace security would come and close the door, locking it.

But no one came.

Josephine hesitated a long moment and then crossed the threshold, leaving her suite for the tower stairs. For another minute she stood at the top of the circular staircase listening. She heard voices coming from below, and then something was being moved or dragged, something heavy.

Josephine carefully went down the stairs to the next floor. The door was wide-open and it looked like a library, a very handsome library with vast bookshelves that rose all the way to the ceiling. Two men in uniform were carrying chairs while a woman ironed the creases from a heavy brocade cloth covering a table that had been placed in the center of the room.

She didn't know if she made a sound or if one of them felt her there, because suddenly they were all nodding and murmuring polite greetings while continuing with their work.

As if she hadn't just been locked away upstairs for days.

As if it was perfectly acceptable for her to wander around the tower.

She continued down the next flight of stairs, wondering if she'd now be stopped, wondering when she'd be told to return to her room, but she passed staff and no one said anything to her or expressed surprise that she was roaming the tower. She peeked into the room on the second floor and discovered an office suite. It was surprisingly sleek and modern, with computers and big screens and stylish leather chairs and lots of steel and plates of glass set into the wall, filling the spaces where a cannon or some other weapon must have once been.

A pretty young woman sat at one of the sleek ebony desks in the corner typing away on a computer. She looked up and nodded at Josephine before continuing with her work.

Everything seemed so ordinary and yet at the same time, everything was extraordinary.

Josephine cleared her throat. "His Highness,

Prince Alexander," she said, her voice not entirely steady.

The young woman looked up again, smiling politely, professionally. "His Highness has arranged for dinner at nine in the library. That is on the third floor, one level up."

"Thank you." And yet still she hesitated, chewing on her lip, trying to process what she was hearing and seeing. It seemed she'd been given freedom. Was this the queen's doing? Or had Alexander changed his mind?

Josephine walked down the last set of stairs to the first floor. She pushed open the cloudy glass door and entered a huge private gym. There were free weights and weight machines, a treadmill, a stationary bike, and another piece of equipment she'd never seen before, and behind all that was a stone wall covered with brown, gray, and dark green bumps.

She looked at the wall hard, trying to understand what the bumps were before walking toward it, letting her fingers trail over a light gray wedge jutting out from the tower wall at her shoulder height.

"It's a climbing wall," Alexander said, behind her.

She turned around to find him standing not far behind her. He was wearing charcoal-colored shorts and a white T-shirt, and his bronzed skin was flushed, his black hair damp. She couldn't help noticing the way his thin T-shirt clung to the planes of his broad chest and the curve of his sinewy biceps.

"I didn't realize you were here. I'm sorry I interrupted your workout," she said.

"I'd stepped out for a moment to take a call," he answered, lifting the hem of his T-shirt to wipe his jaw, revealing his hard, flat abdomen with his chiseled abs. "But you're not interrupting. I'm just about finished."

She heard the words but couldn't focus on them, suddenly transfixed by the glimpse of his chest, reminded of how that lean, hard torso had felt against her. Her gaze dropped to his hips just before he dropped his shirt, covering himself, but she remembered him there, too, and how his body had given her such pleasure.

Josephine swallowed hard and averted her gaze, but it was too late. Heat rushed through her and she felt tingly and exposed, even as a deep craving hit her, making her ache for the feel and weight of him. "It's an impressive gym," she said hoarsely.

"You're welcome to use it anytime."

She didn't want the gym, though. She wanted him. And the unbidden thought made her loathe herself because she shouldn't be so weak. She shouldn't still want him, not after everything that had transpired. "Your mother came to see me just a little bit ago," she said, struggling to distract herself. "Was that how my door was left unlocked?"

"It's been unlocked for the past two days."

"It hasn't."

"It has."

"But that scraping sound—the lock turning…"

"It's just the hardware. It's old. It should be replaced."

"You let me think I was locked in."

"I did."

"That's horrible. You should be ashamed."

"I am."

"You don't sound it. If anything, you seem rather pleased with yourself."

"I'm pleased to see you."

Her lip compressed and she glanced away, but not before her gaze swept over him, focusing on his midsection, seeing yet again that lovely hard torso in her mind's eye.

She'd been fascinated by him before they'd ever met. She'd watched him on the beach, interested in only him. She'd filled her sketchbook with his likeness.

He was her weakness.

And yet she felt increasingly vulnerable, and not at all safe. "I'm afraid this isn't going to work," she said, her voice low and husky. "And I don't know how to make it work since I no longer trust you."

"I'll earn your trust back."

"I don't think—"

"You have to give it a chance, Josephine."

"It will take time."

"Yes, it will. Unfortunately, it's the one thing we're short on, and so I ask you to trust me that the trust will grow."

"Alexander."

"We need to marry soon—as in right away. As it is the baby will be born early, and we can fudge a few weeks, but every day it will become harder to hide the facts of his or her conception. I can handle gossip. I'm accustomed to slights and insults, but I don't want there to be excessive speculation about our child's birth. Nothing should mar his or her future. Life is hard enough without being born under a cloud of doubt."

Finally, he'd said something she agreed with. Life was hard, and no child should have to grow up with any stigma or gossip surrounding him or her. "Do you even like children?" she asked.

"What a strange question."

"I think it's a fair question. You had never mentioned them before."

"Before? You mean on Khronos when I didn't know my name or where I came from or even my native tongue?"

She squirmed inwardly, thinking he'd made a fair point. "You never asked me how I felt about becoming a mother. You never asked me my feelings on anything."

"I'm sorry."

She shot him a narrowed glance. "So my bedroom door will remain unlocked?"

"Yes."

"You're giving me my freedom back?"

"Freedom to explore the palace grounds, yes."

"But not beyond?"

"You may leave to explore Roche provided you have ample security. But I warn you, it won't be the same as before. The people know you're here—"

"How?"

"I'm followed constantly, *cara*. When I leave these castle walls, I'm followed and photographed and everything I do and eat and buy is documented. Which is why I've kept you here, on the inside. I'm trying to buy you time, giving you a chance to mentally adjust to the changes taking place."

She was silent a long moment. "I don't have very much control anymore, do I?"

"No."

"Or very many options."

"Unfortunately, no."

"What options do I have? What am I allowed to decide?"

"The time of day you'd like to be married. The choice of venue for the ceremony—the chapel here,

within the palace grounds, or the Gothic cathedral
on Roche's historic square."

He added in the same flat, unemotional voice,
"You can choose the type of reception we will
have. You have absolute control over the wedding
details, large and small. You can decide where we
will honeymoon—"

"I don't want a honeymoon."

"You don't think it would be good for us to get
away and have some time alone?"

"I've had time alone with you. And look at me
now."

A possessive heat flickered in his blue gaze and
the edge of his mouth lifted in a sensual curl. "I'd
like a week with you where you don't have to cook
or wait on me. I'd like to do nothing but keep you
in bed all day."

She felt the curl of his lip as darts of sensation
raced from the tips of her breasts through her belly
to between her thighs. "I think we did that, too."

"There are so many things I want to do with
you—"

"No, thank you."

"You'd enjoy it."

"Just like I enjoyed being locked in your tower?"

He considered her words. "Bondage is a form of
foreplay. I find the idea of tying you up, or maybe
handcuffing you to the bed, very erotic. I think
you would, too."

Her pulse leaped. Heat stormed her cheeks. "You clearly don't know me, not if you think I'd enjoy being handcuffed or tied up."

"You don't know that until we try."

She'd never imagined such a thing, and yet she could see herself naked, tied to her bed, waiting for him. Waiting on him. It was shocking and yet thrilling. A frisson of raw desire, spiked by nervous excitement, shivered up and down her spine. "You are being blatantly sexual," she murmured huskily.

His gaze slowly roved her face, lingering on her lips. "You like me blatantly sexual."

"You made me sexual."

His broad shoulders shrugged. "Chemistry has never been our problem. We work. We make sense. Why? I don't know. You're the scientist. You tell me."

Her breath caught in her throat as heat and awareness surged through her. It had been almost three weeks since they'd been intimate and yet her body remembered him and ached for him to hold her down and make her his again. She could remember his lips at her neck and the roughness of his chest against her breasts and the thickness of his hard, hot shaft entering and filling her. When he was with her, in her, she felt unbearably good... She felt complete.

And part of her desperately wanted him again.

CHAPTER SEVEN

THEY WERE TO have dinner in his tower library that night. Alexander had given his staff instructions to set a proper table and provide a proper meal with a proper dessert, and since he had a few minutes before dinner, he stopped by his father's room.

The king's butler opened the door to Alexander. "He's awake," the butler said. "But he's not in the best of tempers."

"Thank you," Alexander replied, grateful, as forewarned was forearmed.

King Bruno was in bed already, and he watched Alexander approach his bed from beneath heavy lids. "You've cleaned up. Who are you trying to impress tonight?"

"I'm having dinner with Josephine."

The king's jaw tightened, his expression closing. When his father said nothing else, Alexander added, "I intend to present her to you tomorrow, Father."

"I'd prefer not."

"I'm aware of that, but she doesn't need to be, and then after I introduce you, I'm moving her into the palace. It will be a short meeting. You won't have to do much—just nod and I'll whisk her out and it will be over."

She wanted his warmth and the sensation of being his, and only his, but another part of her knew he wasn't good for her. Her desire made her dependent. Her desire clouded her thinking. She struggled to remember why they were at odds, needing to create distance, needing a form of defense. "But it's changed," she said breathlessly. "We did have chemistry, but that was before, back when we were on Khronos. When I felt safe with you. I don't anymore."

"You will again."

"So I can go out? I can resume normal living?"

He took so long to answer that she dreaded the answer. "It won't ever be the normal you knew before," he said at length, "but yes, you can go out, and yes, you can go shopping, or out for a meal. But it will be choreographed at our end. Palace security will want to know the details so they can have a plan, create a route, and ensure your outing will be as stress free as they can make it."

"My normal isn't shopping and restaurants. My normal is home. My work. The beach."

"You will have work. It will just be different—"

"Is that supposed to appease me?"

"No. I'm being honest. I think it's better if we lay all the cards on the table. The truth is you will have a new life here, and you will have a new normal, and I promise that I will do everything in my power to help you settle in so that you can be happy, eventually."

A new life here.

A new normal.

Be happy...eventually.

The words echoed in her head. She raised a hand to her face, fingertips pressing against her forehead where pain throbbed. She didn't want a new normal, and she didn't want a new home, but none of that seemed to matter, and honestly, she had no one to blame but herself. She'd lost her head on Khronos. She'd thrown caution to the wind. They'd made love a dozen times. Risks had consequences and the consequence was that they'd created a new life.

She dropped her hand, looked up at him. "Does anyone even know about me?"

"They know you rescued me after my...accident. They know you saved my life, and they believe you're here to be thanked by my parents."

She frowned as a troubling thought came to her. "What about the pregnancy? Does anyone know about that?"

"No. It's a closely guarded secret. Only four people know you are pregnant: our parents and the doctor who performed the ultrasound, and I'm determined that no one else know, not until we choose to make an announcement, most likely once you are well into your second trimester."

"Who is *we*? The palace, or you and me?"

"It will be up to us, I promise."

Up to us. *Us.*

"Don't you think I should meet both of your parents before I say yes?" she asked, taking a deep breath. "I realize your father is the king, but he will be the grandfather of my child. I want to be sure he approves of...me." *Us.*

Alexander hesitated. "My father can be difficult."

"Is that your way of saying I should lower my expectations?"

He smiled crookedly. "You're quite good at subtext."

"I heard that you and Damian had a falling-out. I hope it's not true."

His father had always been more interested in Damian than him. "We're fine."

"Why hasn't he come around, then?"

"I wondered the same thing."

"He's always been very loyal to me."

"Just as I have, Father."

But Bruno had no response to that, choosing to close his eyes, ending the conversation.

In the tower library, iron-and-glass wall sconces had been lit so that the room glowed with red and gold light. A ruby brocade cloth covered the round dining table and the stemware had ruby-colored crystal stems. The walls of books added to the richness, and Josephine found herself relaxing as they were presented with their second course.

"You will meet my father tomorrow before lunch," Alexander said. "I cannot predict how he will behave."

"You have a difficult relationship?"

"It's been tense since I was a very young boy."

"Is he that hard to please?"

"He's quite pleased with my mother."

"How have you disappointed him?"

"I'm too cerebral. He would have preferred a son more like my cousin, Damian. Damian is physical, shrewd, and aggressive. My father admires a man who will lay down the law and command."

"How are you not commanding?"

Alexander smiled, and then his smile faded. "Josephine, we might never be who we were on Khronos, but that doesn't mean we can't be happy and that we can't create a strong and loving family for this child and any others we choose to have."

"Would you want more?"

"I would like more."

"Because you need an heir and a spare?"

"Because I was an only child and was often lonely. I would love my son or daughter to have siblings, brothers and sisters to play with. Why grow up in a castle if you have no one to chase you up and down stairwells, or play hide-and-seek with in the dungeon?"

She swallowed hard, unaccountably moved by his words. "Your nannies didn't play with you?"

"How can a nanny ever be a substitute for a brother? Nannies don't whisper secrets and share dreams."

Josephine hated the lump filling her throat. She didn't want to care for him; she didn't want to feel connected, and yet his words made her heart ache. She understood better than he knew. She had grown up alone and lonely. She had grown up wishing for a playmate, someone to talk to late at night, someone to wake up with in the morning, someone who would go on an adventure with her. Instead, she'd spent her life entertaining herself. She'd spent her childhood trying to pretend she didn't need anyone.

"You want our child but you don't want me," she said after a moment. "I think that is the most difficult part for me. And maybe it sounds selfish—"

"But I do want you. I want you very much. I locked you here, trapping you in my home, to keep you from leaving."

"To keep your unborn child here."

"To keep *you* here, Josephine." He signaled for the table steward to leave, and once the door closed, leaving the two of them alone, he said, "I still don't have all of my memory. It hasn't completely returned," he added. "It's incomplete, and there are areas of my life that still have…blanks. I know things because people have told me things, but I have no memory of them."

"Such as?"

"The trip with my friends on the yacht."

"Is that all?"

"The first day or two on Khronos."

"You were recovering from an injury. I'm not surprised you're having difficulty with those memories."

"But I was on the yacht for a week before the accident. That's essentially nine days I don't remember, plus the week where I had amnesia."

"What do the doctors say?"

"I haven't told them."

"Why not?"

"Because I'm worried it would get back to my mother, and she has enough to deal with at the moment."

"Is there more I don't know?"

"My father is dying," he said bluntly. "He has lung cancer. It's stage four now. The radiation and chemotherapy have stopped. There is no more prolonging his life. The only thing that can be done is to try to make him as comfortable as possible—and that's not working."

"And this is why you keep saying we're running out of time. Because you literally are running out of time."

He nodded. "I want my father there when we marry…if humanly possible."

"But why didn't you just tell me? I would have better understood the pressure and urgency."

"Because this is how families like mine operate. We're royals. We maintain facades. We keep up appearances. We're not supposed to have problems. We're not supposed to struggle. And to accomplish that, we suppress anything that is remotely problematic—"

"Like emotions?"

His lips curved wryly. "Indeed, emotions are terribly dangerous."

"I think living without emotions is dangerous."

"Says the woman who loves volcanoes and lava."

"Don't forget plumes of ash."

"How could I?" He hesitated, gathering his thoughts. "We don't do *dramatic* here. And we don't have volatility in the palace. It's all very contained and controlled."

"That's dreadful."

He hesitated. "It can be."

"So who knows about your father?"

"Just a handful of us. Those who must know."

"Rather like my pregnancy."

"But that will be good news, just as our wedding will be good news. I know my mother is hoping our happy news will help soften the public's grief when they learn of my father's cancer."

Josephine swallowed hard, her mouth going dry. "That's a lot of pressure."

"I've grown up in a fishbowl. You're being thrown into it. But I have faith in you. You're a strong swimmer."

His gaze held hers, and there was something in his eyes, as well as the gruffness in his tone, that made her feel tender. She pressed her hand to her chest, pushing against her heart. "Thank goodness I like the water."

He rose and left his chair, and once standing next to her, he reached into his coat and withdrew a small velvet box. As he lifted the lid, he knelt at her side. "Josephine, would you do me the honor of marrying me and becoming my wife and future queen?"

She looked from the huge ring in the box—a massive square-cut emerald surrounded by layers of diamonds—up into his face. He was so very handsome and yet so very aloof. In Khronos he'd been relaxed and physical, and she suspected that in bed he'd be just as sensual here, but she worried that there was no room for emotion. She wondered if he'd ever loved a woman. She wondered if he'd ever love her.

His mouth tugged into a reluctant smile. "I'd hope you would say yes."

She flushed. "Yes, it is a yes. I'm sorry."

"Don't be sorry. Just give me your hand."

Mortified, she held her hand out to him and he slid the ornate ring on her fourth finger. It was loose and slid sideways. She shifted it around, struck by the weight of it.

"We'll get it sized tomorrow," he said, rising.

Josephine couldn't look away from the immense emerald. "It's beautiful."

"It's an Alberici family heirloom, from the early nineteenth century."

She balled her hand to keep the ring from slipping sideways again. "Your world is overwhelming."

"Trust me, I understand."

"I never wanted to be a princess…not ever, not even as a young girl playing make-believe. I loved fables, not fairy tales. I identified with animals, not villagers."

"I never wanted to be a prince," he said, taking his seat at the table again. "As a boy I rebelled against my birth. I didn't want to be nobility. I didn't want to be privileged. My father thrashed me for being ungrateful and undeserving of my position, and I learned never to voice my concerns or objections again."

"It must have been quite a thrashing to have permanently silenced you."

"The thrashing wasn't that bad, but being sent away from home was. Although I imagine it would have happened sooner or later."

"Do you remember it still?"

"The conversation with my father, or the punishment?"

"Both, I suppose."

Alexander leaned back in his chair. "I remember the conversation because I felt very pleased with myself. Rather righteous, if you will. You see, from a young age I'd been uncomfortable with royal protocol, almost cringing when government officials and the public bowed to me, thinking I'd done nothing to earn their loyalty and deference. I didn't think it fair that I was simply born with advantages. It wasn't egalitarian."

"Oh, dear, I can see that being problematic if your father was as old-fashioned as you say."

"Mmm. How dare I be a populist?"

"And you, his only child."

"An embarrassment to the Alberici name." Alexander smiled wryly. "I'm sure I didn't help things by pointing out to my father that the monarchy was a huge expense for the people of Aargau, costing over two hundred million euros a year to support the monarchy here, and yes, a portion comes from the Alberici estate, but didn't an equal portion come from the Aargau government, which was really from the taxes the people pay?"

"You didn't."

"I did."

"And then what happened?"

"Thrashed, sent to my room without food or water for the night, and then the very next day I was packed up and shipped off to a military academy where the staff was told to turn me into a proper man."

"I would think that was an invitation for abuse."

"For someone raised outside society, you understand it very well."

"I read a lot."

He reached across the table to fill her glass with more sparkling water. "I remained at the academy until I was seventeen, then served three years in the Royal Navy and was finally allowed to attend university at twenty. I escaped Europe for four years in New Haven, Connecticut, where I studied philosophy, economics, and environmental science before returning to Europe to earn a graduate degree from Cambridge in land economy, a field that combined environment, law, and economics."

"That's why your English is so good."

"I confess, I liked living overseas and loved my time in America. You have a freedom we don't have here. It's probably why I took a job in Paris after my graduate degree. I wasn't ready to come back to Aargau and be Prince Alexander. I liked being one of the people."

"You don't think you can be one of the people as your country's king?"

"Not the way I was raised."

"Then when it's your turn, do it differently so that our son or daughter can embrace a future in which he or she has the opportunity to be happy."

"I would encourage a career, then."

"Your father didn't have one?"

"From the age of eighteen he has been king."

"He has done his duty, then."

"Yes."

"And when it is your turn, you will do your duty, too."

The meeting with his father was short and rather brusque, but Alexander admired Josephine's calm and gracious manner even under fire. His father spoke barely a dozen words to her, but at least those words included curt approval granting them permission to marry.

Queen Serena didn't speak until the end, but once her husband had given his blessing for the marriage, she rose and gave both Alexander and Josephine a kiss on the cheek. "Congratulations," she murmured. "And welcome to the family," she added to Josephine.

The meeting lasted barely five minutes and they were done, exiting the room with Josephine's hand tucked into the crook of his arm. Her hand was trembling. He'd had no idea she was nervous until then.

He glanced down at her bent head as the doors to his father's room closed behind them. Her thick, light brown hair with the streaks of blond had been pulled back in a stylish twist. She was wearing a simple navy dress paired with navy heels. Small pearl drop earrings dangled from her earlobes. "You look very elegant," he said quietly, trying to distract her from the hollow ring of their footsteps on the marble floor. "Have I seen this dress before?"

She reached up and touched the matching strand of pearls at her neck. "No." Worry darkened her green eyes. "Your mother sent the dress, shoes, and jewelry to me this morning. She said I was probably wishing I had something chic for my presentation and hoped the dress and shoes would help me feel suitably prepared."

He was surprised, but then again not. His mother excelled at soothing and smoothing tension. And yet she was no pushover. His mother was probably the strongest woman he knew. "I wish I had thought of that. You do need a new wardrobe. And an assistant. I will have a team meet with you after lunch."

"I don't need an assistant or a new wardrobe, and I have this dress now in case I need to see your father again."

He stopped on the bottom marble stair. "I don't think you realize what is about to happen. Our engagement is being announced this afternoon. We will soon become the focus of the press and a great deal of speculation, particularly when we announce the wedding is just a week from Saturday."

"Nine days from now?"

"It's not a lot of time, no, which is why we'll have a little preparty next week, either Tuesday or Wednesday, to celebrate our good news—"

"Is that really necessary?"

"We must do something or people will find it odd that I've kept you locked away—"

He broke off as she arched a brow. He laughed softly. "You will never let me forget I locked you up, will you?"

"Absolutely not. You're terrifying. I should call you Bluebeard."

He smiled and kissed her, and then again, his lips lingering against her mouth. She shivered against him, her hands pressed to his chest. "You're too good at this," she murmured. "You make me almost want to be locked up with you."

"I knew it," he said. "Now, where are my hand-cuffs?"

"Easy does it, Your Highness. We're not even married yet."

"True, and speaking of marriage, I think it'd be wise to make some decisions so my mother won't worry."

"Can't we just make some decisions now and tell her?"

"Do you know what you want?"

"Small wedding, only our immediate family—yours, and my father. I'd like it to be a quick service, if possible, so that it's not too much for King Bruno. Afterward cake and a toast with our parents and then, later, a private romantic dinner for just you and me."

"That's not a very proper royal wedding."

"We both know I'm not a proper royal bride."

CHAPTER EIGHT

WHEN ALEXANDER HAD said that the palace would begin the wedding preparations immediately and that Josephine's days would quickly become tightly scheduled, he hadn't been exaggerating. She'd expected some appointments and anticipated some meetings, but her entire life was taken over. She also quickly discovered that future princesses lived anything but private lives.

Within an hour of the engagement being announced, she was surrounded by staff. There were women at her side who were assistants managing her schedule, with others managing her wardrobe, while others had tasks she didn't yet understand.

It only took a few days of constant companionship to make her miss her tower bedroom, which was far from the bustle of the palace. She missed her view of the sea, which reminded her of Khronos, her father, and the work that had been such a passion for so many years.

She also struggled with the sheer number of women who surrounded her now, women who all had corrections for her. They coached her on how to walk, how to carry herself, how to speak. How to hold her knife and fork. How to lift a glass. How to place a teacup. How to sit. How to rise.

How not to cross her legs. How to hold her head. How to smile. How not to smile. And how never, ever to laugh.

The hours of daily instruction were meant to help her. The instruction was meant to help shape her into a proper princess. But all the lessons in etiquette and deportment, all the correction of her grammar, all the jabs at her posture simply made her feel pathetically inadequate. Every moment of her life had become a teachable moment, and for someone who'd been homeschooled and who had done her learning through stacks of books, the very vocal, critical coaching was an excruciating reminder that she was a problem. A *mistake*.

More than once she overheard her ladies murmuring about the difficulty in shaping her into a lady before the party on Tuesday, where she'd be presented to various members of the aristocracy, family friends, and a selection of Aargau's Parliament.

In addition to the lessons, there were fittings and more fittings, and she was tired of standing still, being measured and draped and discussed as if she were a headless mannequin.

In the last four days she'd been pricked with more pins than she cared to remember. She noticed there were no trousers for her and nothing remotely slouchy or comfortable being made. Everything was expertly tailored: scooped necklines, snug belts, skirts with demure hemlines. But the fabrics were gorgeous and every finished item was beyond luxurious.

Alexander appeared at her room one afternoon, interrupting a meeting with Lady Adina, who was again going over the guest list for Tuesday's party with her, ensuring that Josephine was indeed familiar with all the names and the correct titles.

No one had heard him enter, and Josephine didn't know how long he'd been standing there, observing them at her writing table. "Hello," she said breathlessly, happy to see him and grateful for the interruption. "Do you need me?"

"No. Not if you're busy."

"We're not that busy," she said, rising, thinking he looked ridiculously handsome in crisp olive trousers and a starched white shirt, the sleeves rolled up on his bronzed forearms. His shirt hugged his shoulders and molded to his chest and narrow waist. Just looking at him she could see why she'd thrown caution to the wind and fallen for him so hard. "And I feel like I haven't seen you in ages."

"I know, and now I'm heading to Paris but I should be back tomorrow."

She looked up quickly, hopeful. "Could I go with you? I've never been to Paris and I'd love to see something new—"

"I wish you could, but last-minute trips are expensive, even without the additional rooms and security we'd need since we're not yet married." He reached for her hand. "Come, walk with me in the picture gallery. I don't think I've taken you there yet, have I?"

"No," she said quietly, feeling flattened.

His fingers laced more fully with hers. He gave her hand a slight squeeze. They walked silently from the room and down the hall. It wasn't until they'd reached the staircase and gone up a floor and then entered a long corridor filled with enormous oil paintings that Alexander stopped walking and faced her.

"I am going to Paris to see one of my friends, Phillipe," he said quietly. "Phillipe was on the yacht with me, and he's leaving for an extended trip to Buenos Aires and I want to catch him before he goes."

"He hasn't tried to see you or reach out to you?"

"He's close with Damian, my cousin. And the fight on the yacht, it was between Damian and me. I think Phillipe has avoided me to avoid having to take sides."

She was silent a moment in order to process what he was saying. "The fight on the yacht... It was between you and your cousin?"

"Yes."

His expression was so grim that she was almost afraid to ask anything else. But she'd been there, on the beach, when he'd gone overboard, and she'd been the one to rescue him. She'd seen the wound on his head. She knew firsthand the damage inflicted. "This is the cousin your father wanted you to be more like."

"We were raised almost like brothers."

"But he was the one that hit you?"

"Apparently in self-defense."

"What? How?"

"I don't know. That's the problem. I only know what I've been told. If only I could remember, but I can't, and so I'm dependent on the memories of those who were there."

"Have you asked to see the footage from the security cameras? The ship must have them. Everyone has them—"

"It was the first thing I asked for on returning home. But it seems there were no cameras at that end of the ship. It was one of the few places that lacked surveillance."

"Strange, don't you think?"

"From what I've learned, I was the aggressor that night. If what is being said is true, my behavior is inexcusable."

"What are they saying you did?"

He shook his head. "I'd rather not."

"And I'd rather hear it from you than from someone else."

"Fair enough." Alexander moved away from her

toward the wall of framed portraits, but he didn't seem to be looking at any of the canvases. "It's all rather complicated, as I'm telling you what Gerard told me took place."

"So Gerard was there? He saw it happen?"

"No, this is what Damian told Gerard."

"I don't find that very reassuring."

Alexander shot her a pensive glance. "According to Damian, he noticed I was missing, and then he noticed Claudia—"

"Who is Claudia?"

"His girlfriend." Alexander swallowed. "And my ex-girlfriend."

Josephine's eyebrows arched but she held her tongue.

"So he went looking for us," Alexander continued, "and found us on the deck off her room. We were having an argument." His jaw tightened. "I had my hands on her. I was threatening her, shaking her, choking her. Damian intervened and rescued her, taking Claudia to get medical care and leaving me alone on her deck."

"How did you go overboard?"

"I don't know."

"No one came to confront you? No one came to kick you out of her room?"

"Gerard came to find me. He said her room was empty."

"Did he then go to your room?"

"Yes, and the door was locked, so he left me alone." Alexander fell silent. "Everyone assumed I'd gone to bed to sleep it off. But when I didn't emerge from the cabin by early afternoon the next day, my friends forced open my door to check and discovered I was gone."

"That's why they never sounded the alarm."

"And why no one knew where to look for me. By early afternoon the yacht had covered a great distance." He drew a breath and forced himself to continue. "What worries me is the fight. The fact that I was shaking her or angry with her. I don't know why I'd be upset. I've never been bothered by her seeing Damian. How could I be? I was the one who ended it with her."

"You think Damian is making all of this up?"

"But why? What purpose would it serve?"

"So you believe him, then? You shook Claudia and choked her, and then you somehow, all on your own, fell off the yacht?"

"People do stupid things when they drink, and I have been told I was drinking heavily that night."

"I'm sorry but none of this makes sense. I've never seen you drink to excess."

"I did, when I was younger, back in my university days. And I had a reputation for being a bit of a hothead when I drank, but that was years ago. Ten years ago. I don't drink like that anymore."

"Tell me about Claudia."

He shot Josephine a sharp glance. "Why?"

"I've never heard you mention her until now and I find it interesting that your ex-girlfriend was on your bachelor trip."

"As my cousin's girlfriend."

"But wasn't that awkward?"

"Claudia is also the younger sister of Marc, one of my best friends. She's been part of my circle forever, which was why I began dating her in the beginning. She knew my world. She understood the rules of my world. She was…convenient."

Josephine didn't know whether she was more shocked, angered, or puzzled. Worse, Alexander's story didn't line up. It wasn't logical. "What were Claudia's injuries?" she asked. "Did the medic on board take photographs? Did she have bruises? Have you spoken to her?"

"Marc, her brother, has told me to stay away from her."

"Is Marc close friends with Damian, too?"

"We met Marc our first year in the military academy. We've been friends with him ever since."

"And Phillipe?" she asked, suppressing a heavy sigh. "How does he fit in?"

"He was another friend from the academy."

"You trust them all? Every last one of them?"

Alexander looked away. He said nothing. His silence ate at her.

She pressed her hands together, fingers interlacing. She was afraid for him. Afraid for both of them. "I'm not trying to play Devil's advocate, Alexander, but something isn't right. I'm worried you've been set up."

He glanced at her, his expression almost bleak. "But what if I did do it?"

She'd been hurt and angry when she'd first arrived in Aargau and locked in the tower, but deep down, she'd always known who he was and what he was. And that was honorable. "I don't believe it. And neither should you."

Alexander's trip to Paris was a waste of time and money. When Alexander arrived at Phillipe's apartment, he discovered Damian was already there. The three of them had dinner together, and on the surface everything was cordial, but conversation was superficial at best. During the meal, they all avoided speaking of the trip. They avoided discussing Alexander's wedding. They actually only spoke of football and the new exclusive VIP club that had just opened up in Paris.

Alexander regretted the trip. He wished he'd remained in Roche with Josephine, and then it crossed his mind that he didn't have to stay. He could leave now and return home tonight. He could return now.

Alexander acted on impulse and rose. "Thank you for dinner, but I should get back. Phillipe,

enjoy Buenos Aires. It's a favorite city of mine."
He nodded at Damian. "I expect I'll see you back
in Roche soon."

"I've been waiting for an invitation to the wedding."

"We're keeping it small and private."

"And the party Tuesday? No invitation for that
one, either?"

"I was going to give it to you in person when you
came to see me at the palace. You haven't come
by. You haven't phoned."

"I was waiting on an apology."

"Ah, I see. Good to know." Alexander tipped his
head and started for the door.

Damian was on his feet and he followed. "You
need to get help, Alex, and if you won't do it on
your own, I'll make sure you do. I'll speak to
your father. I'll go to Parliament. I'll take it to the
media."

Alexander turned around. "Why make it public?
What do you hope to accomplish?"

"You'll no longer be able to avoid the truth—
that you're not well, and potentially unfit to rule
in your current condition."

Alexander regarded his cousin a long moment
and then nodded. "Good to know." And then he
walked out, grateful for the car waiting for him
downstairs and the private jet that could fly him
home tonight.

* * *

Josephine hated being at the palace without Alexander. She felt trapped and bullied, although she suspected Alexander wouldn't understand because he'd grown up here and he'd been raised to conform. But it wasn't just the constant critical company that wore on her; it was her boring, uninspiring routine. She could only hope that once the wedding was over she'd be given more space, as well as more control over her day. Until then, she'd have to stand at windows, looking out, waiting for Alexander to find her and make her feel safe and wanted again. He was the only reason she was here in Aargau. Her hand went to her belly and she cradled it protectively. Well, Alexander and this one. Her baby.

In the beginning she'd been nervous about the pregnancy, but now she was excited, and determined to be a great mother. Josephine had been raised by a single father, and while he'd loved her, he'd never quite managed to be both mother and father. As a little girl, she'd desperately missed her mother, and that ache for a mother had never gone away. Even now, maybe particularly now due to the pregnancy, Josephine longed for a mother to talk to her, give her advice, and reassure her. Fathers were good at many things, but they didn't carry the baby, and they didn't deliver the baby, or nurse, or do any of those other things, and what Jo needed now was a strong maternal figure to help her adjust...

or even some knowledgeable girlfriends would do. She hoped that later Queen Serena could maybe become that figure, but until then, Josephine would continue being her own best friend.

On Sunday afternoon, Alexander walked the castle parapet with the stunning views of Roche's medieval walled town against the brilliant blue of the sea. Damian's words haunted him. He'd returned from Paris in the middle of the night, and it had taken him hours to fall asleep, deeply troubled by the tense meal as well as perplexed by Damian's threats.

This wasn't the Damian Alexander knew. This Damian was bitter, with a score to settle.

Was it really about Claudia? Or was there something else that had happened, something that Alexander couldn't remember?

He closed his eyes and drew a deep breath, and in his mind's eye he saw Josephine, lovely, warm, smiling.

He was glad she wasn't Danielle—sleekly sophisticated and coolly polished—and he didn't want anyone to try to make her into something she wasn't, because he liked her the way she was. He liked everything about her. She was the woman he wanted, and she'd be a good queen even if she hadn't been raised in his world. Maybe she'd be a better queen because she hadn't.

He wished he'd taken her to Paris yesterday. He

wished they had more time together, just the two of them. Maybe he should steal her from the palace and take her for a drive. They could run away for a couple of hours, just the two of them. They could escape in one of his cars, perhaps one of the convertibles, and drive, the wind in their hair, the open road before them.

Alexander stopped pacing, the idea cementing. He knew where he'd take her, too. It would be an hour drive, but it was a beautiful one, across the middle of the country, through picturesque villages, all the way to the country's highest point, Mount Bravura. But if they were to do it, he'd need to put the plan in motion now.

Alexander made a call to Julio Costa, the owner of the restaurant, and then went in search of Josephine. His valet was the one who told him to look in the tower guest suite.

When his valet saw his surprise, he smiled faintly. "Miss Robb likes it there," he said. "Everyone knows it's her favorite place to go when she needs a break from her ladies."

This drew Alexander short. "Are her ladies difficult?"

"I think they're excessively preoccupied with rules and protocol."

Alexander left the palace for the tower and climbed to the fourth floor. When he entered the tower bedroom he found Josephine standing on a stool before the tall, narrow window. She was barefoot and her chin was propped in her hand, her elbow resting on the thick stone ledge.

"What are you thinking about?" he asked.

Alexander's voice caught her by surprise. She jumped a little as she glanced over her shoulder at him. "Nothing much," she answered.

"Your *nothing much* is always something."

The corners of her lips lifted. She turned back to the window and gestured to the horizon. "I was thinking the ocean from here looks more green than blue, and those puffy white clouds, cumulus clouds, are casting moving shadows on the water, making the sea look as if it's filled with a fleet of ships, all at full sail. I was imagining the adventures those brave voyagers would have."

"You make me want to be one of those brave voyagers."

"But then who'd be king? This kingdom has but one heir, which is you."

A half-dozen different responses came to mind and in the end he chose none of them. "I should have taken you with me last night. I didn't enjoy Paris without you."

"How did it go with Phillipe?"

"Not well." He hesitated. "Damian was there."

One of her winged eyebrows arched higher. "You didn't expect to see him, did you?"

"No. And it was an awkward meal. I left early."

"And your cousin? How was he?"

"Baffling," Alexander said after a long moment. "I don't understand it. I don't understand him." And then he shrugged impatiently. "Let's not discuss him anymore. He ruined my night. I won't allow him to ruin today, and I'm organizing something fun for us for dinner tonight. It will be just the two of us. We'll leave here at six. Our reservation is for seven."

Josephine studied him a long moment, trying to read his expression because he wasn't smiling and yet there was this curious light in his eyes. He looked tired but also eager, and she suddenly pictured him as a boy and thought how lovely he must have been. He wouldn't have been one of those who hurt things and broke things. No, he would have been smart and thoughtful and kind. "I'm looking forward to it," she said, and she meant it.

"Good."

"How should I dress? Do I need one of my formal dresses that require the spandex girdle beneath?"

"That sounds horrendous."

"It feels horrendous."

"Then no, please don't wear one. Be comfortable. Choose a dress that makes you happy."

Josephine went through her wardrobe and in the end chose a ruby-red silk dress that was sleeveless, fitted through the waist, and featured a stunning bright pink flower on the full skirt. The neckline plunged, showing off her tan and her curves, making her feel gorgeous and feminine.

After saying good-night to her staff, she hurried downstairs, where Alexander was waiting by the front door for her. He smiled as she came down the steps. "You look stunning."

Pleasure filled her. She felt stunning tonight. "And you're very dashing in your…um…trousers and…shirt."

He laughed, the sound low and husky and unbearably sexy as the butler opened the front door for them. "I'm rather boring—is that it?"

"Actually, no. You're anything but boring," she said as they stepped outside. Her attention was immediately drawn to the hunter green convertible sports car parked in the drive. It was low and sleek with a handsome cream interior. It was also a two-seater, which meant no room for a driver. "Is that for us?"

"It is. Do you approve?"

"Very much so. But where will your security go?"

"Security will be behind us, but they're to be discreet and give us some room."

"I love it, but I think I might need a shawl for the way home. Let me run back up. I won't be long."

"I can have someone fetch you something—"

"No need. I won't be but a moment." Josephine went back inside and up the marble staircase.

She'd just opened the door to the suite when she heard one of her ladies say, "They said Damian found them together on the yacht, in her room, in her bed. He confronted them and things turned ugly. It's why Damian has been forbidden from coming here."

Josephine froze, unable to make herself move.

"Not surprised about the love triangle. There has always been some friction between those two," someone said.

"It doesn't help that the king has always favored Damian over his own son."

"And Claudia? Where is Claudia now?"

"Paris, I believe."

Josephine felt sick. Her legs shook. She put a hand to the wall, trying to steady herself. Was it true, what her ladies-in-waiting were saying? Had Alexander gone to Paris not to see Phillipe but to see Claudia?

Was it possible that Alexander wasn't who she thought he was?

Closing her eyes, she pictured him downstairs waiting for her next to the sleek sports car, handsome, smiling.

She pictured him as he was when he came to her in the tower…

She remembered how he'd pulled her aside to talk to her in the picture gallery…

Had he been lying to her all those times? Had

he been twisting the truth, pretending to be someone he wasn't?

She didn't think so. Maybe she was crazy, but she trusted him. She did.

Josephine drew a breath and pushed the door all the way open, silencing the conversation as she stepped into her sitting room. She ignored the startled glances—as well as the fact that the ladies were sitting in her sitting room—and continued on to her bedroom.

Adina jumped up. "Did you forget something?" she asked, following Josephine into the bedroom.

Josephine counted to ten as she went through her wraps and then selected a charcoal-gray pashmina and draped it over her arm. "I have it now," she said, turning around and heading back out. She didn't pause until she reached the door to the corridor, and then she glanced back at the three women. "If you're going to gossip, please do not do it in my rooms. Good night."

For the first twenty minutes of the drive, Josephine was quiet, replaying the conversation she'd heard in her room, wondering if she should tell him. She didn't want to spoil the night, and it would certainly spoil the night. She chewed on the inside of her lip, wishing she hadn't gone back to her room, thinking she would be so much happier right now if she'd never heard any of that.

Alexander shifted and glanced at her. "Is my driving making you nervous?"

"No. Just thinking about something I heard earlier. It was disturbing."

"Want to tell me?"

"No." She swallowed around the lump in her throat. "I'm just upset on your behalf."

He shifted again and braked, pulling off on the side of the road. Alexander faced her. "Tell me, *cara*. We're in this together. Let's do this together."

"People are talking," she said quietly after a moment. "Staff. They're saying you…" She closed her eyes, shook her head. "I can't say it. I can't. And I don't believe it, so it doesn't matter."

"But it does matter because clearly it's upset you."

She opened her eyes. "They're saying on the yacht, Damian found you…in bed…with Claudia."

"What?"

"And that's why Damian is angry."

"No."

"And Claudia is in… Paris." She looked at him. "Tell me it's just a coincidence. Tell me you didn't go to Paris to see her—"

"Absolutely not. I didn't even know she was in Paris. Furthermore, we weren't in bed together. I can promise you that. And yes, I know I have memory issues, but there has been nothing between Claudia and me since I ended the relationship, and I haven't wanted to be with her. I might not remember the trip, but I know me, and I wouldn't start something with her again, not when she's involved with my cousin. I hate even discussing Claudia with you, but you must believe me—"

"I do." She reached out, her fingers light on his cheekbone and then his jaw. "I do. I'm just disgusted by the gossip. I'm disgusted that people in the palace would speak that way about you."

"Damian grew up in the palace. His father, Aldo, was my father's twin. I think Damian has always struggled with the fact that my father was born two minutes before his father, making my father the future king and me the heir instead of the other way around."

"Damian resents you."

"I think Damian is envious, yes."

"That explains a great deal," she murmured, leaning forward to kiss him. "But let's not let Damian and his green-eyed jealousy ruin our evening, because I'm so happy being out with you. Let's just savor our night."

"I couldn't agree more."

Now outside the city, they turned off the main highway onto a narrower rural road, and for the next half hour they threaded their way through the countryside filled with farms and little stone houses with charming shutters and window boxes.

Josephine thought it looked like a blend of Provence and Tuscany. "It's so picturesque," she said as they slowed for a shepherd and his flock of sheep, the fluffy creatures slowly crossing the road just ahead of them and then deciding they no longer wanted to cross the road but instead mill about, taking over the road.

"We might be a while," Alexander said, shifting into Neutral.

"I'm enjoying myself immensely," she replied, delighted by the herd's inability to decide if they'd all cross together or one at a time. She entertained Alexander with a sheep-by-sheep accounting, describing the wayward members of the flock, giving them all personalities, including the shepherd, whose quiet resignation coupled with his inability to direct his flock only served to make the sheep more ambivalent about crossing the road in the first place.

"He is not a very good shepherd," Alexander muttered, as five minutes turned to ten.

"Not terribly passionate about his work," she agreed, "but he's giving me the best show."

"He's also going to make us late for dinner."

She glanced at him. "Is that going to be a problem?"

"No. It's Sunday, and Julio is opening the restaurant specially for us."

"I've never had anyone open anything for me."

"Well, you will now. In just five days you'll be Princess Josephine Alberici."

The sun was just setting by the time they pulled

in front of the restaurant, with its exterior of local wood and stone. The restaurant owner, Julio, warmly welcomed them before escorting them inside to a table in an alcove with windows all around. The view from the restaurant, which happened to be perched on the edge of a cliff, was nothing short of glorious.

"We're up so high," Josephine said.

"It's Mount Bravura, the highest peak in Aargau and Aargau's only volcano, although extinct now."

"No wonder I like it so much!"

They drifted into easy conversation, interrupted only by the waiter when he took their order and then returned later with their first course. Time passed quickly, and Josephine was surprised when she sat back and glanced out the window and found it was pitch-dark and that the restaurant itself was empty save them and the owner. "It must be late," she said. "All the staff has gone."

"Even Julio?"

"No, he's still here. He's setting the tables for tomorrow."

"I'm sure he'd have no problem kicking me out when he's ready to go home."

She frowned, skeptical. "Even though you are Prince Alexander Alberici?"

He laughed lowly. "Okay, Julio would probably never kick me out, but he's thrilled we're here. Tomorrow he'll share the news with everyone and he'll get a great deal of press out of this. His bookings will double, triple overnight."

"Well, that does make me feel a little better, but I still wouldn't mind stepping out for fresh air."

"Because you're tired or because you want Julio to be able to close his restaurant and go home for the night?"

"You know me so well," she murmured, thinking Alexander had the loveliest blue eyes and his smile created these grooves on either side of his lips. Lightly she brushed a fingertip across his mouth, wanting more than a light kiss. She missed the heat between them. She missed the tension and electric sensation.

He rose and held her chair for her. They left the restaurant for the patio with its breathtaking view. It was only up here, so high, that Josephine got a sense of the island and its size. Lights twinkled far away—the capital of Roche, Josephine thought— with other lights dotting the coast. Waves crested with white reflected the moonlight.

"This was just what I needed," she said with a sigh. "It almost feels like we're on Khronos. It's just you and me."

"You miss Khronos."

"I think I always will. I had so much freedom, and I miss the water everywhere." She darted a look up at him. "And I miss having it be just you and me."

He leaned against the railing and drew her to him, his hands low on her back. "You have no idea how much I've missed you. I want to feel you and love you. It's been too long."

Love her, Josephine repeated silently, even as her heart did a painful double beat. She knew he didn't mean love, *real* love, but still, it was heady hearing the words and knowing he desired her— and at least desire was something. Maybe desire could be enough. Maybe she could be satisfied with being wanted. Maybe she didn't need to be loved. Or maybe her love for him would be enough for both of them.

She stared deep into his eyes, flooded with so many intense emotions, emotions that were stronger than she'd ever felt before, and then, sure of her feelings, she leaned closer, leaning into him, and pressed her lips to his. "It has been too long," she whispered against his mouth. "I need you to love me."

He kissed her back, his hand cupping the back of her head, drawing her against him so that her breasts pressed against his hard chest and her mouth was his for the taking.

The kiss was fierce and hot, his tongue parting her lips, sweeping her mouth before tangling with her tongue, teasing it, teasing her.

She felt as if the kiss was just the beginning of something huge and wonderful and she mimicked the way he kissed her, sucking on the tip of his tongue, drawing on it hard. He groaned against her mouth, his hands sliding down her back to grip her hips and grind her against his hard length.

Her arms wrapped around his neck, her fingers twining in the dark strands of hair at his nape. She tugged at them even as he shifted her hips, drawing her over him again, making her feel his heat and hunger. Sensation flooded her. Emotion flooded her. She'd desired him on Khronos, but it was so much more intense now, her feelings making the need and sensation so much more powerful.

His tongue played her mouth in a rhythmic stabbing that mimicked how the thick head of his shaft pressed up between her thighs. He'd found her breast with one hand and was kneading the peaked nipple, making her whimper and shudder, and if it weren't for the fact that security was just around the corner and Julio was somewhere inside the restaurant, she would have begged him to take her here and now, as the delicate silk of her dress gave her little protection. But then, she wanted no protection. She wanted him, all of him, forever.

He lifted his head. "I'd have my way with you right here if I didn't think it'd make Julio feel awkward."

She laughed and blushed. "I was just thinking the same thing. Can we go back home and be together?"

"Absolutely."

They returned to the palace and he led her to his room. They made love twice, and she spent the rest of the night barely sleeping because she didn't want to forget how good she felt in his arms, in his bed.

CHAPTER NINE

Tuesday, with its cocktail party of important people and influential guests, had finally arrived, and Josephine's team spent hours preparing her, giving her a complete makeover. The hairdresser, makeup artist, and stylist fussed over her for nearly two hours but now she was dressed and waiting for Alexander to collect her.

Josephine did a little twirl before her mirror, absolutely thrilled with her dress. The sleeveless gown featured a dramatic V neckline, with a soft cloud of a skirt shimmering with gorgeous gold embroidery. The skirt floated around her legs as she walked and she was wearing glittering chandelier earrings from the Alberici vault. With her hair pinned up, she definitely looked older and more sophisticated.

Alexander arrived exactly on time to escort her to the ballroom, and when he entered her room she expected him to smile and compliment her because it's what he usually did, but tonight he kept his distance and stared at her, jaw flexed, gaze shuttered. Her ladies-in-waiting noticed, too, and they fell silent. The silence grew, making Josephine uncomfortable.

"Something's wrong," Josephine said quietly. "Is it the dress? Would you like me to change?"

"The dress is beautiful."

"Then what is it?"

"I'm having a difficult time understanding why you look so different. I don't understand what has been done to you. You don't look like you."

She remembered the hours of tortured hair-styling and makeup application and lifted a hand self-consciously to her nape, which was exposed tonight, with all her hair coiled and pinned tightly on top. "It might be this style," she said. "It's structured."

"Too structured. It doesn't suit you. You are too pretty to look like an old lady." He approached her and reached out to tip up her chin, examining her makeup. "You're wearing quite a lot, aren't you?"

"The eyeliner is rather heavy, and the lipstick is dark," she said faintly.

"Why didn't you stop them?"

"I was told they'd been instructed to polish me, remove the hard edges."

"There were no hard edges. You're lovely as you are."

His words made her eyes sting and it was all she could do to keep tears from welling up. She glanced at the women in the corner who were hanging on every word and she gave them a faint smile before looking up at Alexander. "Please don't be disappointed. They've been working very hard to prepare me for tonight—"

"You are not a rock," he gritted out, interrupting her. "You do not require polishing or refinement, and if this is what they're telling you, then I will throw them all out, every last one of them, because I like you, and I want you to look like you. I want your mouth to look like your mouth. I want to be able to kiss your lips—" And then suddenly his head dropped and his mouth slanted over hers, and he was kissing her with hunger and passion, as if they were alone.

By the time he lifted his head, ending the kiss, her head was spinning and her senses swam with the erotic pleasure of his kiss. She loved his mouth on hers. She loved the feel of him and the smell of him and the way he made her feel every single time he touched her.

For a moment she just stared up at him, dazed, and then he reached up and began tugging the pins out of her hair one by one. "The public will like you," he growled, his deep voice humming through her. "The public will love you. You don't need to be someone you're not, and you most definitely do not need to be a puppet on a string." He kept pulling out pins until her thick hair fell over her shoulders in long, loose waves. "This is better," he said, combing his fingers through the waves. "This is you, and how I like to see you."

He turned and faced the ladies in the corner. "Do not put her hair up unless Josephine asks for it to be up. Do not apply more makeup than she is comfortable with. Ask her what she wants—do not tell her. Am I clear?"

Josephine was simultaneously awed and horrified. "They will not like me better for that," she whispered, trying not to smile as she wiped away the lipstick staining his mouth.

He turned his head and kissed her palm. "Maybe not, *bella*, but I will."

They were only a few minutes late arriving for the party in the ballroom, and while Alexander had assured her it was an intimate gathering, the fact that they were going to the ballroom spoke volumes.

As the doors opened to admit them, Josephine's breath caught in her throat, and her fingers tightened on his arm as she was immediately dazzled by the splendor of the grand ballroom. Her appreciative gaze swept the space, trying to process everything she was seeing even as people began bowing to Alexander. Immense chandeliers ran the length of the high ceiling, each dripping with glittering crystals, reflecting shimmering light across the elegant baroque ballroom, enhancing the gold and white scheme where gilt-framed mirrors lined the walls.

"Confidence," Alexander murmured at her side.

She eased her grip on his arm and forced a smile, trying to block out the sheer number of people filling the room. There were so many people here, and they were all staring. "This is not a small party," she whispered as his hand slipped to her lower back.

"It's fewer than three hundred," he answered under his breath. "Larger than I hoped but small compared to the usual number we host for formal gatherings." He began introducing her to people, a couple here and a couple there.

She nodded, smiled, and spoke when required, but the entire time she was most conscious of *him*. His warmth filled her and his fragrance teased her nose. Even though she was uneasy with the sheer number of people present, she felt safe with him, reassured by him at her side. There was something in his touch that made her skin come alive. She loved it. She hated it. He was never supposed to be hers, and yet here she was, being introduced to his court as his bride-to-be.

"You're doing well," he murmured when they had a moment to themselves. "You're quite impressive actually. You'll be the princess they adore, and before long their queen."

She glanced up, her gaze meeting his, his irises almost lavender blue in the glittering light. She wanted to tell him she loved him. She wanted him to know how much she cared about him and that she didn't need the public to love her, as long as he did.

Later, as they mingled, she found herself watching him, and she knew he was also watching her. She could feel his gaze on her, and he made her feel so many things—taut, edgy, physical, desirable.

Tonight, everything in her felt sensitive and alive, especially when he looked at her, as he did just now, his lids lowered and his lovely mouth lifted just so, and she felt that half smile all the way through her, the awareness making her skin warm and her body tingle and ache.

Tonight she felt unbearably feminine, all curves and softness. Her breasts. Her waist. Her hips. Her thighs.

She loved everything about him. She loved the way he moved, she loved watching his hands, loved the width of his shoulders. She watched his eyes, the focus, the intensity, the hint of amusement lurking there in the light blue gaze.

Perhaps she wasn't a mistake.

Perhaps she was the right bride.

The party was a success. Photographs of Prince Alexander and his beautiful young fiancée, Josephine Robb, filled the papers, and Josephine could tell from the smiles of the staff that everyone was pleased.

Josephine was pleased, not because the party was a success but because the party was over. She couldn't wait to escape the palace the next afternoon, retreating almost immediately after lunch for the tower bedroom where she could be alone with her favorite view of the water.

She waved at Alexander's secretary, Aimee, on the second floor as she hurried up the stairwell, and then she peeked through the open door to the library and saw Alexander there in a chair reading a thick sheath of papers. She nearly spoke to him but then thought better of it because he was lost in thought, and she raced on up, feeling immeasurably lighter and happier.

The formal party was over. The wedding was coming on Saturday, and then soon the spotlight should be off her, and she and Alexander could develop their own routine and their own life together.

She couldn't wait for them to be a proper family, and she wondered where they'd raise the baby. She was trying to imagine the nursery when she moved too quickly, misjudging the distance between the stone steps. Josephine flung her arm out to brace her fall but it was too late to stop herself, and she screamed as she fell, crying out again as she slammed onto the stairs, the impact knocking the air out of her.

For a moment she lay dazed, and then she pushed herself up into a sitting position. She flexed her hands, tested her legs. Nothing seemed broken. She ached though, with pain in her torso and a wrenched back.

"What happened?" Alexander demanded, charging up the stairs, coming to her side.

"I fell," she answered, trying not to wince, not wanting to alarm him. "I was distracted and lost in thought and my feet ended up going faster than the rest of me."

"You could have been seriously hurt," he said.

"I know. But I wasn't." She allowed him to help her to her feet but she frowned at the twinge in her belly.

"What's wrong?" he asked.

She forced a smile, hiding her pain, thinking now wasn't the time to be melodramatic. She'd just taken a fall, and by most standards it was a very small fall. She hadn't even gone down more than five or so stairs. Everything was fine. She was certain everything was fine. "Just a bit stiff from falling. Your stairs are hard," she added lightly, trying to tease him to ease the tension.

"You shouldn't be coming up here. It's a very old staircase, the steps far too narrow and steep. My mother mentioned they were dangerous years ago—"

"I've never fallen before, and next time I'll go more slowly. I promise."

"There won't be a next time. The tower is off-limits."

"Stop it! You're being ridiculous. I'm fine. Look at me—" She broke off to wiggle her fingers and flex an ankle. "No cuts. Nothing is broken."

"I'm taking you back to your suite in the palace."

"You don't need to take me anywhere, Alexander. I can walk just fine."

"I'll feel better if I see you there."

"Fine."

He held her hand as they started down, and she could tell by the firm clasp of his fingers that he was trying hard not to lift her up and carry her the rest of the way. She was touched by his concern. It was a little heavy-handed, but he'd always been protective.

She was just about to thank him for his assistance when she felt another twinge in her abdomen, sharper, much sharper than before. Startled, she paused on the step and suddenly she had to look at Alexander. Suddenly she needed to hear from him that everything was okay.

"Something is wrong," he said roughly. "Don't tell me everything is fine."

"It's pinching on the inside. It's getting stronger."

"Where?"

She put her hand on her still-flat belly. "Here," she whispered, cupping her womb. "Where the baby is."

He muttered an oath and swung her into his arms. "Let's get you to your room and we'll call the doctor from there."

She was in bed when the doctor arrived, but she'd been to the bathroom twice because she'd noticed she'd begun spotting. She was trying to contain her panic as she added pads to her panties, trying to tell herself that this was just a little blip and everything would be fine.

But as the doctor drew out the fetal Doppler to listen for a heartbeat, her eyes burned and then filled with tears because she could see from Alexander's tense expression just how concerned he was.

They were all quiet as the doctor listened. An hour ago she'd been so happy, almost elated that everything she wanted was finally coming together. But now Alexander stood just behind the doctor, silent, watching and waiting.

When the doctor put the Doppler away and made a call for someone at the hospital to bring over an ultrasound, her heart fell.

"You don't hear anything, do you?" she said, her throat constricting.

"You're still quite early. It can be difficult listening for a heartbeat with a Doppler. The ultrasound will allow me to have a better view, and we'll be able to see the heart beat."

Alexander was thanking him but Josephine closed her eyes and turned her face away, unable to let them see her fear because something was wrong. She felt it. She knew it. From the cramping to the bleeding to the doctor's nonexpression, the professional kindness intended to mask concern.

The nurse arrived with the equipment in just

thirty minutes but the doctor's silence as he studied the ultrasound image crushed her. She knew.

She knew.

"There is no heartbeat," he said quietly. "I am so sorry."

For a moment she couldn't breathe. For a moment she felt as if she'd just vanish into thin air.

There was no heartbeat.

The little life inside her was gone.

She shook her head, and then again, unable to look at the doctor or Alexander. This time when she turned to face the wall, she stayed that way, even after the doctor and his nurse had gone.

She gripped her hands into fists, trying to keep from screaming. This was her fault. All her fault.

"Josephine," Alexander said, putting a hand on her shoulder.

She shrugged him off. "Don't say anything."

"I know what you're thinking," he said. "I know what you're saying to yourself, and it was such a little mistake, such a simple thing."

"Please go. Please leave." She squeezed her eyes shut, fighting the scalding tears.

"The doctor wants us to go into his office for the procedure he mentioned—"

"I don't want to do it."

"I know, and I don't want you to be put through it, either, but he believes it will be better for you, less risk of an infection."

"Alexander, no."

"I hate this, too, *cara*, but we need to keep you well. We need to do what's best for you now."

The procedure on Wednesday night was horrendous, and Josephine slept in on Thursday, having cried herself to sleep the night before.

She didn't want breakfast Thursday morning, and she didn't want to get up, too spent, worn-out, wrung out, cried out. Queen Serena came by her room just before noon to tell her how deeply sorry she was, and shared that she understood Josephine's grief because she had miscarried, too, and that Josephine should feel free to come to her anytime, for anything.

Josephine got through the short visit without breaking down, but once Serena had gone, she curled into a ball and cried again. The last six weeks had been a gigantic roller coaster and this last drop was too much, too frightening, too heartbreaking.

Worse, there was no reason for Alexander to marry her anymore. He was only marrying her because of the baby, but now that there was no baby he was free.

She'd freed him. That was good, right? Still crying, she threw back her covers and got out of bed. She should go. That's what she should do. She should just go and put this whole nightmare behind her.

Josephine was in the middle of packing the few things she'd brought with her when Alexander entered her room. From his expression, she knew that someone from her staff had alerted him that Josephine was preparing to leave.

"What are you doing?" he asked quietly, taking in the clothes she'd put in the pile to leave at the palace and the sarong and blouse and swimsuit she would take back to Greece with her.

She wiped tears away. "I want to see my father. I want to be in my house again."

"Your father is on his way here for the wedding."

"We're not getting married now," she said, folding another simple blouse. "There is no reason for him to come."

He crossed the room and closed the door that divided the bedroom from the sitting room where her staff had collected. "You can't run away every time there is a problem," he said tersely, facing her. "You have to be stronger than your fear."

"I think there is some confusion here. I'm not afraid. I'm just no longer necessary, which is why I'm choosing to return home."

"Not necessary? You're my fiancée. My intended. My betrothed. We've announced it to the world. We've celebrated it in style. We have a wedding in two days."

"It's a small wedding, a very private wedding. It's not going to be difficult to cancel it."

"I don't understand. I know you're upset about the miscarriage, but why are you doing this to us?"

"Because there is no *us*!" she cried, balling up a T-shirt and smashing it against her knees. "There has never been an *us*. This—" she gestured to him, and then herself "—this has never been about you and me. It's only been about the baby, and the baby is no more."

"You are my fiancée. We're marrying in two days."

"Why? You don't need me. You don't want me. You were only marrying me because I was pregnant, and I'm not pregnant anymore. You're free. Go! Find Danielle. Or find a new princess. Find someone who wants to be your princess. I never wanted the job." She rose and stepped over the clothes, wishing she could fling the doors open and escape, but there was no escape here, and there would be no escape, not until she was on her own island, in her own world.

"I am not going to break off our engagement." His voice was hard, every word sharp and brittle. "I cannot put my father through the humiliation of another broken engagement. It would kill him—"

"He's going to die anyway!"

"How dare you?" He took an enraged step toward her and then stopped himself. "How dare you disrespect him—"

"I'm not trying to disrespect him, Alexander."

Her voice broke. "I'm trying to save us from disaster. You don't love me. You desire me. You've sexualized me. But there is nothing else for me… There is no real relationship. I'm to be in your bed, and at your side for important appearances, but what else is there for me? Why should I stay? Give me one good reason to stay!" She was almost trembling with emotion, trembling with the need to hear him say he loved her and wanted her above all else—not because she was pregnant and not because this was duty but because he couldn't live without her. He didn't want to live without her.

"Because you made a promise," he ground out, jaw flexed, blue gaze icy. "My father has given us permission, and we have announced our wedding, and I will not disappoint my father again. I refuse to disappoint my father. I will not."

They weren't the words she needed. Her eyes burned, filling with tears. "So you'll trap me and disappoint me."

"You benefit, *cara*, you benefit beautifully from this arrangement."

"No."

"And there will be children. You will be pregnant again soon—"

"I knew you were not a terribly sensitive man, but your lack of empathy at the moment is astonishing."

"My lack of empathy? My father is dying—"

"And my child just died." Her voice broke and she reached up to knock away the tears, hating them and hating him. He had no idea how much he was hurting her. He had no idea how every word he said wounded. "And I appreciate that your father is a king and I am but an ordinary woman, an American at that, but can you please allow me to grieve for what I have lost? Or are you too self-absorbed with duty and your tortured relationship with your father to allow me time to mourn and heal?"

She'd finally effectively silenced him.

He stood there stiffly, features granite hard, no emotion anywhere on his handsome face.

She should have felt a thrill of victory because she knew that finally something she'd said had penetrated his thick skull and the even thicker wall he kept around his emotions. But she hated that it was the miscarriage that should do it. How much better if he'd actually loved her. How much better if he'd been willing to fight for her.

Alexander saw the pain in Josephine's eyes and her pain unnerved him. She was so open and so vulnerable and he could see what she was feeling—even feel what she was feeling—but the sheer intensity of so much emotion made him shut down and pull even further away.

Emotions had always been problematic for him, but his father's death was even more challenging because this was his last chance to get it right.

This was Alexander's last chance to try to make amends with a father who had never wanted or needed him. If there ever was a time to be the son Bruno had wanted and needed, it was now. "I am not indifferent," he said lowly, his voice rough to his own ears. "I am more disappointed than I can say—"

"I don't believe you."

He gave her a slight bow. "I'm sorry."

Her eyes welled with tears. "Let me go."

"No." *Never.*

"You don't need me—"

"But I do." *Always.*

"Those are just words!"

But words didn't come easily to him, either.

What he longed to do was take her in his arms. He wanted to hold her and comfort her, but his own control was being tested. He was battling to keep it all together. He hated what was happening to them, and yet there were bigger things than their own personal drama.

"We will get through this," he added quietly. "I promise."

"You disappoint me," she whispered, averting her face.

He flinched but said nothing.

She blinked hard, adding, "I kept thinking we had a shot at making a marriage work. I thought that there was something real between us. But I was wrong. There is no *us* in your world—there is just you. It's your world, your title, your future… not mine. It was never mine."

She was wrong. There was an *us*, but he didn't have the energy to argue, and so he stopped focusing on Josephine's words, unable to take them in. He'd been mocked for his feelings as a boy. He'd been brutalized in the boarding school by other boys because he'd dared to care…to hurt.

In the navy, he'd been drilled to be tough. Feelings, once again, had been shameful. They made a man weak when he needed to be clearheaded and logical and strong.

So no, he wouldn't feel her pain, and no, he wouldn't let her words register because it would do no good. Her pain and disappointment would change nothing.

His father was dying.

The country would need a new king.

His mother would be widowed and displaced.

Alexander needed to do now what he'd been raised to do. Shoulder the weight of Aargau. Do right by the crown. Honor his father's memory and name.

He didn't know why he'd been on the yacht near Khronos, and he didn't know what had happened on that yacht or why she'd been there to save him, but it had happened and they were now here, and everything was about to change.

Josephine might not like what was happening, but she'd rise to the occasion. He knew she would. Just as he'd known she'd do the right thing by their child.

Josephine understood honor. And in her own way, she understood responsibility and duty. She'd be an excellent queen one day. He just wished the path could be less painful.

"You can return to Khronos after the wedding," he said. "You can take some time once we're married. I will speak with the security—"

"No. Not after. There is no after—"

"Josephine, stop for a moment. Think carefully, please. Look at the bigger picture, if you can."

"You mean you and what you want?" she flashed bitterly.

He ground his teeth together. She didn't understand that he was trying to do the right thing now, which was give his father peace of mind so King Bruno could let go of this life and the pain racking his body. Because his father wouldn't let go, not if he believed the family was in crisis.

His gut hurt. His throat felt thick. Alexander forced the words out because they were not easy to speak. "My father is a fighter. My father has lived his life for his country and his duty. But he's in constant pain, terrible pain, and he's ready to go. The only thing he lives for now is seeing us married. But if that doesn't happen, he'll try to cling to life, which will only increase his suffering. We must protect him from pain. He mustn't think we are in crisis. He needs us to be strong, *cara*. I need you to be strong. I am sorry I've hurt you, and I'm sorry to have disappointed you, but consider him. Consider my mother. They need us to show courage and leadership now. They need to know the monarchy isn't in crisis and that you and I are unified and committed to Aargau."

She stood utterly still, chin lifted, eyes shimmering with tears. She stared at him so long he could see the pulse beating at her throat and the faint quiver of her lips.

Anger blazed in her eyes. Hurt created shadows, too.

"I wish you'd never come to Khronos," she said at last, her voice hoarse. "I wish I'd never seen your yacht anchored in the cove or watched you and your friends on my beach. I wish I had amnesia. I wish I could blank out the entire thing so I didn't have to remember it, either."

He winced inwardly. They were sharp words and they pricked, like shards of glass scraping across his skin.

"I thank God every day because you are what I woke to," he answered gruffly. "I thank God that you were there, grateful that you are here. We will get through this. We are a strong family, and you are part of us now. There is no crisis here. You are hurt and upset, but you belong here. You belong with me. There is no running away. We are out of options and out of time. We will do what needs to be done. You and me, together."

She looked away, her pale throat working, her eyes blinking as she tried to contain her emotions. She'd been through a great deal in the past twenty-four hours, but they couldn't give up now. His father needed peace. The wedding would go ahead as planned, and eventually all would be well. Storms passed, skies cleared. Josephine would get pregnant again, and there would be a royal heir; Alexander didn't doubt it, which was why he could walk out of her room and go to his father's side and assure him all was well and they were looking forward to the wedding on Saturday.

CHAPTER TEN

HE DIDN'T WANT the truth, and he didn't want her emotions. He didn't want her to feel.

So she wouldn't feel. And she wouldn't care about him any longer. She'd do her duty. She'd marry him and stand at his side and fulfill the obligation, and then she'd leave.

She'd return to Khronos and stay there, not for a visit but until her father took a new position with the foundation and was sent elsewhere. She'd go where he went and continue assisting his work. She'd lose herself in the work, and the idea of going somewhere pleased her. She imagined a return to Washington State, or possibly Peru, or maybe even to Mount Etna in Sicily because she'd never feel the same about Khronos. Alexander had ruined it for her.

On Saturday morning Josephine was numb as her staff dressed her. The wedding was a late-morning service, designed to accommodate King Bruno as he was at his best in the morning and wouldn't be too groggy from the heavy-duty pain medicines he took at noon.

Josephine's gown looked like something from a fairy tale. She was reminded of Cinderella at the ball, except her dress was white, with a big tulle skirt, a sweetheart neckline, and an impossibly long train. Her long sleeves were sheer and her lace veil was attached to a delicate tiara, the veil as long as her dramatic train.

The hairstylist curled her hair and left it down in long, loose curls, and the makeup artist took forty minutes trying to cover Josephine's pallor and make her look fresh and dewy instead of heartbroken.

Her ladies escorted her down the stairs to the palace front steps where a special carriage waited. Her father stood next to the carriage in his formal wear looking nervous, and yet his expression cleared as he caught sight of her. "You look so lovely, Josephine," he said, reaching for her hands and giving them a squeeze. "And so very much like your mother. I wish she could be here to see you. She'd be so proud."

Josephine was glad now she hadn't told him about losing the baby, or her anger, or the fact that she'd soon be returning to Khronos. She'd give him this moment. He deserved the moment. "I think Mama is here," Josephine whispered.

Her father wasn't a sentimental man, but his eyes glistened. "She wanted the best for you, but I'm sure she never imagined you here, about to become a princess."

Josephine couldn't answer and was grateful when the royal page opened the carriage door, and her father assisted her up the steps. Her ladies lifted her skirt and long lace veil, and then they were seated together and the door closed. The carriage was off.

The ride to the cathedral on the square should have been short but crowds had lined the sides of the street, hundreds of people, no, thousands, coming out to witness Josephine dressed to marry their prince. They cheered for her, time and again, and she blinked repeatedly, fighting tears, touched by the cheers and the shouts of *Princess Josephine! Princess Josephine!* not expecting such a welcome.

The cheers and nerves all became a blur once she reached the cathedral. Her ladies were there again, somehow making it to the square before the carriage, and once again they straightened her dress and veil and handed her flowers from the carriage, flowers she had somehow missed before.

The walk down the cathedral aisle was endless. Sunlight poured through the tall, arched stained glass windows. The soaring ceiling provided the perfect acoustics for the organ. She knew the classical piece being played. It was Mozart. Her mother loved classical music. The thought gave her comfort as she approached the altar. She spotted Alexander there at the very front, standing next to the robed priest. He was dressed in his Royal Navy uniform, the jacket black, the thick shoulders covered with ropes of gold. He had medals across his chest, and with his black hair combed severely back, he looked tall and powerful, virile and handsome.

Part of her thrilled that he was hers, and another part couldn't forgive him for not loving her. Today should have been joyous, not a duty to be borne.

Reaching his side, her father placed her hand in Alexander's and then stepped back to take his place in the front pew.

She felt Alexander's gaze bore into her but she wouldn't look at him. She just wanted to get the service over and the formalities completed so she could take this gorgeous fairy-tale dress off and remove the delicate, sparkling diamond tiara—a tiara she'd been told was worth millions of euros—because although she was marrying Alexander, she hadn't grown up on fairy tales and she no longer wanted to be his princess.

The drive back to the palace was stiff but not quiet as the crowd chanted their approval, the cheers like thunder as Alexander traveled in the carriage with Josephine.

She lifted her hand and waved to the crowds, smiling when she spotted a sign with her name, but she never once looked at him.

He told himself he didn't mind, but he did. He actually minded a great deal. And so he focused on other things, turning from Josephine's elegant profile, and how beautiful she looked in her lovely gown, to nod and wave to the crowd.

He'd done what he needed to do today. He'd married, and one day in the future there would be another baby, the heir, and his father could return to his room and his bed, and take his medicine, and escape his pain.

"I think we will save the cake and champagne for later this afternoon," he said as the coach passed through the palace gates. "Let my father rest and my mother relax, and then we'll meet before dinner and have a toast before your father goes home."

She turned her head then and looked him in the eye. "Yes, Your Highness."

"Josephine."

"You got what you wanted, Alexander. Your father can rest easy now. But please don't expect me to celebrate."

Josephine had just finished changing into a slim skirt and elegant blouse—her new official royal uniform, it seemed—when a knock sounded on her door. It was one of her ladies, and she was in tears.

"He's gone," she choked. "King Bruno is dead."

That day there was no celebratory cake or champagne. Indeed, the entire wedding was eclipsed by the death of Aargau's beloved king. The shocked public immediately went into mourning.

Josephine herself didn't know what to feel. On one hand, she was glad the king was no longer suffering, but she felt for Serena and for Alexander. They had been expecting his death but not quite so soon.

Perhaps it was better it had happened so suddenly.

Perhaps it was best that it had happened today as it shifted the focus from the newlywed couple to the funeral for the late king.

Josephine's father returned to Khronos and Josephine kept to her rooms, or when she did go out, she walked the safe paths on the castle grounds, going from the rose garden to the orangery and then through the vegetable garden and the orchard.

Alexander did not come to her, and she did not seek him out.

His mother, though, was another matter, and Josephine took to spending a half hour in the queen's chamber every afternoon after her garden walk, either reading or attempting to do some needlework. She was terrible at needlework but her efforts seemed to please Serena, and so she tried. Serena would have tea served and the two of them would pretend to eat one of the cakes that accompanied the tea tray. During their time together, Serena did not mention her son and Josephine did not bring him up. Sometimes Serena would say something about the funeral plans—the funeral now just days away—and Josephine would nod and listen, because Serena seemed to need that.

Josephine needed someone to talk to as well, but the ladies surrounding her were employees, staff members, not friends. It would have helped to have a friend in the palace. Someone Josephine trusted, someone Josephine could ask for advice, because clearly Alexander had no need of her, not anymore. He was much in demand, busy planning funerals and coronations. Why did he need her now? He didn't. She resolved that the day after the funeral, she'd go. She wouldn't make a fuss. She'd slip away. It was the best way to handle the goodbye since they weren't exactly her strength and Alexander wouldn't pursue her. Alexander no longer needed her.

Alexander was in his tower office at his desk when his secretary approached, letting him know that he had a visitor.

"It's Claudia," his secretary said. "I've taken her upstairs to the library. I thought it better than in the palace."

"Thank you," he said, rising and heading for the stairs.

Claudia was pacing the library when he entered. "I wasn't sure you'd see me."

"Why wouldn't I?"

"You've avoided all of us since the trip."

"Gerard told me you'd left Roche for a while."

He hesitated. "Someone else said you've been in Paris."

"I've been in Zurich, not Paris." She looked at him hard. "I thought I'd hear from you, though. I was sure I would. I even left my number with your secretary in case you wanted to speak to me. But when you didn't, I began to worry."

He arched a brow. "Worry about what?"

Her relief gave way to wariness. "You don't remember the fight on the trip, do you?"

"Why would you say that?"

Claudia sat down in one of the winged chairs. "Because I keep thinking, if you remembered what happened, you would have taken action. But you've done nothing, at least not as far as I can see, and I've been on tenterhooks waiting for you to reach out to me."

When he said nothing, she added, "I'm not trying to cause a problem, but I keep thinking, something's not right. This just isn't like you."

He drew a slow breath, telling himself not to react. "What should I have done?"

Her brow creased. "Then? Or now?"

Alexander hated not remembering; he hated the blank spots in his memory. "Both."

"I think this is the wrong place to start the conversation. I think we need to back up and I need to say that you weren't rough with me. You were never rough with me in any way, at any time. You do know that, don't you?"

He clasped his hands tightly behind his back, not trusting himself to speak. Why was Claudia here? What did she want? Was this a trick? Was she going to ask for money?

"I don't know what game Damian is playing with you, Alex, but you weren't drinking that night, and you didn't hurt me." Her voice broke. "*He* did. You saved me. You found us on my balcony and you tried to help me and he clubbed you with the lantern." She gasped for air. "I ran away terrified, and I've been terrified every day since."

Alexander didn't even realize he'd been holding his breath until little spots danced before his eyes. He exhaled roughly. "Why?" he ground out.

"Because I thought he'd killed you, and I was so afraid he'd kill me. And then when you were found, I was afraid he'd try to silence me. I've been hiding from him. Hiding from everyone, but I can't live like this. I can't avoid him forever."

"Why were you two fighting that night?"

"He thought I was flirting with you. He can't stand it if I speak to you or look at you. He's so jealous of you. You must know that. You have everything he ever wanted—"

"He was always like a brother to me. Growing up, he was always saving me from the worst fights."

"That's not true, either. He was behind those fights and behind those beatings. He always arrived after you were beat up and bloody, didn't he?" Her voice quavered. "Did you ever wonder how he always just happened to be there when you were getting the snot kicked out of you? It was because he paid the other boys to beat you up. He paid them so that he could come and look like the hero when actually all they'd done was what he longed to do—hurt you."

"What do you want from me? Money? A couple hundred thousand euros? What is it, Claudia?"

"I just want to be safe. That's why I'm leaving. I have my own money, and friends in Vancouver, but I needed you to know the truth. I couldn't just go and have you think that you are any way responsible for what happened on that trip."

"I'm not a monster, then," he said under his breath, but Claudia had heard him.

"A monster, Alex? Never. You've always been my hero!"

Aimee saw Claudia out and Alexander paced his room for a moment, trying to process everything he'd just learned.

He hadn't hurt Claudia. He hadn't betrayed anyone. He hadn't failed anyone—with the exception of Josephine, then.

He swallowed hard at that thought because he had failed her, and she was the one who deserved his love and loyalty the most.

Alexander returned to the palace to find Josephine, but when he reached her room, she was gone. One of her ladies said that Josephine might be in the garden as she liked the garden, especially in the latter part of the afternoon. He hadn't known that. He thought he should have known it.

He walked through the rose garden and then the orangery, ending up in the kitchen garden where he found her sitting on a bench beneath a peach tree.

She looked up at him without a smile. She looked at him as if he were a stranger. His gut tightened. They'd become strangers since the wedding.

"Can I help you with something?" she asked coolly, formally.

He wanted to kiss her, touch her, love her, make her his again. Instead he stood there stiffly, aware of the staff probably watching, aware of the security cameras in every corner. He wanted her desperately, but life in the palace was not for intimacy. It was a stifling world, filled with rules and formalities and never-ending protocol.

"I wanted to tell you," he said gruffly, "that Claudia came to see me this afternoon." He frowned, uncertain how to explain everything Claudia had told him. "She said she suspected I didn't remember what happened on the yacht and thought I should know."

"What happened on the yacht?"

"There was a fight, but it was between Damian and Claudia."

"So why were you the one in the water?"

"Claudia said I intervened, saving her from

Damian when he became physical." He felt Josephine's gaze bore through him. Did she doubt him? Or did she doubt Claudia? He wished he knew. "Damian grabbed a lantern and struck me with it. Claudia ran away, afraid, and she's said nothing about the incident because she's afraid Damian might turn on her."

"That must be a relief for you to know."

Alexander hesitated, flashing back to how they were on Khronos. How simple life had been and how happy he'd felt with her. Happy and free. She'd been happy, too.

He struggled with the words. "I also just want to tell you I'm sorry. I'm sorry for dragging you into all of this. I'm sorry for forcing you into a marriage you clearly didn't want—"

"Good. You should be sorry," she said, rising. "You did force me into this marriage, and yes, you can be incredibly selfish, but I'm not surprised you went to Claudia's aid. It's what you would do. You understand responsibility. You never fail to do your duty." And then she walked past him, her skirt brushing him as she headed back to her suite.

Josephine entered her bedroom and carefully closed the bedroom door. She lay on her bed trembling. She had no fight left in her, no fight at all. It was time for her to go. Time to leave. Thank goodness King Bruno's funeral was in the morning. She'd pack tonight and be ready to go as soon as they returned from the service.

The funeral was held in the same cathedral as their wedding. The cathedral was packed with kings and princes, and political leaders from all over the world. The service was long, with prayers and songs from the choir, and two speakers—Alexander and his cousin Damian.

Alexander spoke first and was eloquent about his father's virtues and his passion for his country, while Damian spoke of his uncle Bruno's vigor and strength and reminisced about the trips they'd taken, the sporting matches they'd played, and how close they'd been, more like father and son than uncle and nephew.

Josephine could see Alexander's jaw tighten and his fist clench as Damian spoke. She found herself watching Alexander's hand and the way his fingers curled and then unfurled. She kept her gaze fixed on Alexander's hand because it was far better than seeing the pain in his face.

Two hours later, Josephine gave her suite of rooms a last glance before lifting her small suitcase and heading for the corridor.

She'd written Alexander a note and she intended to put it on his bed. But as she approached his suite, she heard voices, and she hesitated outside the door to his living room, not wanting to interrupt.

But one of the voices grew louder, the tone menacing. "You think because your father is gone I won't tell the Parliament what you've done? You think I'm going to protect you when you're a violent, unpredictable man, not fit to lead this country or wear the crown?"

Josephine shivered a little, recognizing the voice as belonging to Damian. But that's not why she shivered. She shivered because she was remembering the yacht and the voices she'd heard the night she'd saved him.

It was the same voice. The same anger. The same delivery, the same inflection.

It was Damian who'd fought with Alexander. Damian who'd struck him.

Fear swamped her, not fear for herself but fear for Alexander, and just like that night on the beach, she couldn't move. She couldn't leave him.

She slowly twisted the doorknob and opened the door just enough to get a look inside. Alexander was sitting in a chair, calm and composed, while Damian paced back and forth.

"I will tell them everything," Damian said. "I will destroy you. I will make sure everyone knows who you really are, and when I'm finished, you will be finished because no one will believe you or trust you, not when they find out you have mental problems and lapses in your memory—"

"Whatever are you talking about?" Josephine interrupted, pushing the door open and entering with a faint smile. "You sound almost…crazy, Damian. I'm surprised because you gave the most moving tribute to King Bruno earlier. Was it all an act? Or is this an act now?"

Alexander was immediately on his feet. "Josephine," he said, a warning in his voice.

She walked toward Damian. "Please explain something," she said, still smiling. "Why do you think people will believe you? What makes you think they won't believe him?"

"Because he's brain damaged. He's lost his memory—"

"Yes, he lost it. But it's back. He's told me everything. I know everything. Shall I fill you in?"

"Josephine," Alexander growled.

She ignored him again, her arms crossed over her chest. "You despise him because he's the heir and you're not. During your trip, you were seething with jealousy because Alexander would soon be king. Not you. Never you. Not as long as he lived. And so you provoked him, hurting Claudia, knowing Alexander would go to her aid. Once Alexander was where you wanted him, you took a lantern—very handy, I might add—and bashed him over the head, and then while he was reeling, you pushed him overboard."

She stood now just in front of him and she practically vibrated with fury. "You thought you'd gotten away with it, too," she added. "You thought you were going to be Aargau's next king. But then Alexander returned, and you lost your big opportunity. You must have been devastated. I can only imagine your pain. I almost—*almost*—feel sorry for you."

Damian stared down at her for long moments before he stepped back and barked a laugh. "That was good. I almost believed you. But you have no proof, he doesn't remember—"

"But he does. He told me everything. How else do you think I know?"

Damian stopped laughing. He glanced from her to Alexander and back. "If he knew, why hasn't he said something? Done something? It's because he's still brain damaged—"

"I'm not brain damaged," Alexander said mildly. "I object to that. But Josephine is right. I told her everything, and she has told her staff everything, and they in turn told security." He walked to Josephine's side and slipped his arm around her waist, holding her tight. "The palace guard has been instructed to arrest you should they find you anywhere near the palace or any member of the royal family again."

"You're lying. You're bluffing," Damian choked, furious. "You can't arrest me because you had no proof, and you'll never have any—"

"The palace guard is here, Your Highness," a voice said from the doorway.

They all turned as Gerard entered with the palace security. "We've heard everything and there is more than enough evidence to convict you," Gerard said shortly.

"But I did nothing! This is all hearsay!" Damian cried.

Gerard shrugged. "I was able to recover the missing security footage. It's all on camera. Every word Josephine said was true."

"But there was no security camera," Damian protested. "I know. I checked her room and balcony carefully."

Silence followed. Gerard gestured for the guards to take him. Panicked, Damien put his hands out. "Wait. I'll leave. I'll leave Roche. I won't come back. I promise—"

"Not just Roche, but Aargau," Alexander said flatly. "You're not welcome here, and should you be found trying to enter Aargau, you will be arrested and charged with crimes against the state. Understood?"

It had been a very long, difficult day, but Alexander was finally alone with Josephine in his bedroom, which was just where he wanted her.

"You saved me twice," he said, sitting down in a chair near the bed and then pulling her onto his lap.

He noticed she'd allowed him to draw her down, but her posture remained ramrod straight. She was still upset. He didn't blame her, but he was also beyond proud of her, and in awe. She was a marvel, a heroine, and she was his.

His hand skimmed over her hair, stroking from the top down. "How am I to live without you?" He didn't give her a chance to answer. "I'm afraid it's impossible, which is why I can't let you go."

Her chin tipped, nose lifting. "You can't make me stay. I'm done being ordered about."

He checked his smile. "Well, then, I'll just have to lock you back in the tower."

She turned her head sharply and glared at him. "Have you learned nothing these past few weeks?"

He lifted one of her long silky curls. "I did. I just told you. You weren't listening. I can't live without you."

"You'll be fine. You're not in danger anymore."

He stroked another curl and then wrapped it around his finger. "Not true. I'm in danger of losing you and it'll break my heart, and what kind of king would I be with a damaged brain and a broken heart?"

She smothered a laugh but he felt her back heave and the inelegant snort made him smile. It felt good to smile. It felt good to have her with him like this. He'd missed her so much.

"You'll be fine without me," she said huskily. "You'll find another princess—"

"Never. You're the only princess I want and the

only woman I love." He turned her head toward him. "I love you, Josephine, I do, and I know I don't deserve you, but I'm asking for a second chance. Let me make things right. Let me prove to you how much I love you and how sorry I am for hurting you—"

"You did hurt me."

"I know I did. I wasn't sensitive about the miscarriage, and I shouldn't have forced you to marry me. I should have let you go home and grieve and come back when you were ready."

She said nothing and he gave her hair another stroke.

"I'm not being honest," he said after a moment. "I'm sorry for what I did, but the truth is I'd do it all over again if I thought I might lose you. I didn't let you go home because I was afraid you wouldn't come back. I demanded you marry me because I couldn't imagine living without you. From the time I was on Khronos, I wanted you, and not just for a few days but forever. There is no one else for me, *cara*, only you."

He tipped her chin up and kissed her lightly. "Tell me we can make this work. Tell me you'll give me another chance. You don't have to love me. You don't have to forgive me. Just promise you'll give me time to get it right, because that has been the one thing we have never had enough of... time. It's always been against us. It's always running out. I need time with you, Josephine, time to prove to you that I can make you happy, and make you feel safe—"

"You do," she whispered, interrupting him. "And you have." She blinked, chasing away tears. "I love you," she added simply. "I have loved you from the moment I saw you on my beach. I was meant to rescue you, just as I was meant to love you. Sometimes I think the only reason I was put on this earth was to be there when you needed me."

"If that's the case, know now that I will always need you, and I will always love you, and I will always want you at my side. We belong together. You, me, and the children we will have."

Her eyes filled with tears. "Do you think we'll be able to have another baby? I want to start a family with you."

He clasped her face and kissed her fiercely. "We will," he murmured a long time later. "I promise we will. Just as I promise you my love and my heart forever."

CHAPTER ELEVEN

THEY WAITED UNTIL the period of mourning was over to take a much-needed honeymoon, and then after the honeymoon there was the coronation with all the pomp and circumstance the crowning of Aargau's new king required.

But finally, thankfully, the guests were gone, and the fuss was over, and life was settling into a pleasant routine at the palace. Alexander would be busy during the days, but he was all hers at night, and they made love with an unending passion and hunger.

But after two months of palace walls and palace views, Josephine longed for a change, and she mentioned to Alexander that she hoped they could sneak away for a few days, or even a day, and do something adventurous and new just the two of them.

She didn't think he was listening, but the next morning while she was having breakfast he strolled into her room and told her that they'd be leaving within the hour.

"What should I wear?" she asked.

"Something comfortable, and bring a sweater or a jacket just in case it gets cold."

Their driver ferried them to the dock, where a

boat was waiting. Josephine glanced nervously at the boat. "Where are we going?"

"It will take us thirty minutes by boat. At this time it's the only way to get there."

"What are the conditions like today?"

"It'll be a little bumpy, but I'll make sure we take it slow."

She nodded and stepped into the speedboat and told herself she wouldn't get seasick and hoped it was true. "Are you going to tell me anything else?" she asked, taking a seat and watching Alexander take one across from her.

"In a bit," he answered. "But for now, just try to relax and enjoy the adventure." He gave her a faint smile. "You like adventures, and freedom. Remember?"

"I do," she agreed cautiously, even as her stomach lurched. She'd been queasier lately, her morning coffee no longer the treat it had once been. And as the speedboat raced across the water, bouncing on some of the bigger waves, sending up a mist of sea spray, she clung to her seat praying she wouldn't throw up.

This was probably not the best adventure when she wasn't feeling well, but Alexander looked so happy that she didn't want to ruin his pleasure.

"Where are we going?" she asked, as the minutes slid by and the boat kept bouncing and she kept swallowing hard.

"There is a bit of rock ahead, nothing too grand. It's barren and remote. But I thought you might like it. I thought you might need a place of your own, a place off the grid with plenty of sun and quiet beaches." His voice had dropped and he gave her a crooked, rather tender smile. "A place where you can be a mermaid and raise our children away from society, noise, and rules and regulations."

Her eyes suddenly stung. Did he know? Did he suspect? She hadn't said anything yet, but she had seen the doctor and he'd confirmed her suspicions. He'd even done an ultrasound and let her watch the tiny, steady, strong heartbeat. "You're describing paradise," she said softly.

"I wouldn't call it paradise, but it is yours, all yours. I'm giving you your very own island."

The speedboat was slowing and yet the wind tangled her hair, and she struggled to push back wild, damp strands from her salt-sticky face. "An island of my own?"

"It's there, ahead of us. Just keep watching the horizon."

She watched and her gaze narrowed as she waited for something to appear. He told her a little more about the island that lay off the coast of Aargau. It was rocky and barren and good for nothing, but it did have a small beach and a tiny little cove, neither of which were used by the public since they had been owned for the past 160 years by the Alberici family.

"So you have been here before?" she asked, leaning forward, thinking she could see a small lump of land in the distance, but not sure.

He shook his head. "I was there once as a boy. My father and Uncle Aldo took Damian and me there for a fishing trip. It wasn't a success, though, and we never returned."

"So you have bad memories of the place?"

"I don't know if they were bad, but they weren't good enough to make me want to return. But it's different now. We're going together."

Yes, it was land ahead of them. It appeared to be a small hill rising from the sea. The island wasn't very big, but then again, it wasn't quite as small as she'd imagined, either. She could see little green from where she sat, and she suspected it was, as he said, nearly all rock.

The motorboat slowed yet again as they approached the shore. The purplish-blue water lightened, turning a shimmering aquamarine as they arrived at the cove, capped by an ivory crescent of sand. The sides of the cove were rocky and relatively high, but the beach was lovely, with its generous swathe of pale ivory sand.

Their boat's driver steered them as close to the shore as he could before turning off the motor. Alexander jumped out of the boat, waded into the surf, and held his arms up to Josephine. "Come, Queen, I'll keep you from getting wet."

"I like the water, remember?"

"Yes, you have gills and fins, I believe."

She laughed as he lifted her from the boat and carried her through the rushing surf to relatively dry, packed sand. Once there, he put her on her feet and together they faced the boat and the view of the sea.

Open water everywhere.

Gorgeous blue sky, a turquoise sea, pale rocks standing sentry at the mouth of the cove, and nothing and no one else for miles until you reached the mainland.

"It's perfect," she said, nodding. "I love it. Is there any place to pitch a tent? Because this is most definitely off grid."

"I thought of that, too. Let me show you what is here and we can see if you think it has potential."

He took her hand and led her toward the back of the beach where it butted against the rocky cliff, and there at the back was a little path carved from the boulders, which actually tunneled back through the rocks.

Josephine felt like she was on a grand adventure as they walked up the path through the small tunnel. She reached out and touched the wall. It was surprisingly smooth. Her lips quirked, wondering at the feat of nature required to make such a tunnel out of what was most likely volcanic rock, and then they emerged into the light, and they'd come to a protected clearing. But it wasn't a true clearing at all as right in the middle sat a small stone house virtually identical to the one she'd called home on Khronos. Josephine's jaw dropped and she looked from the cottage to Alexander and back again.

Same stone. Same shape. Same placement of windows and doors.

She walked quickly to the house, and as she crossed the threshold she felt a jolt of recognition—rough-hewn beams across the ceiling, a big stone hearth dominating the center room, and two bedrooms, although as she inspected both, she discovered that the master bedroom was the one at the front, where Jo's had been, and the one at the back had been divided into two, with a cradle and bunk beds, as if anticipating quite a brood.

"This is my house," she said, doing a slow circle, trying to take it all in.

"I had it copied as closely as I could," he said, arms folded across his chest, a faint smile curving his lips. "The contractor and builders wanted to add more amenities but I refused. I told them it was meant to be rustic and an escape from civilization as we know it."

"You gave me my home back," she whispered, her voice breaking.

"With all the solar-efficient technology we could

find," he said, exiting the house and heading to the back where a pretty trellis concealed a tidy grid of solar panels, tubing, and equipment. "Solar power for heating and electricity. Solar-powered communication. Enough energy to run your own little lab of computers as well, if you should so desire. And last but not least, your own desalination system for as much fresh water as you, and your future garden, desire."

She shook her head, incredibly touched and overwhelmed by the thought and effort that had gone into creating this world for her.

From the beach, this was a deserted island, and yet tucked behind the safety of the rocks was a little house ready for her to come play house. "You make me feel like Marie Antoinette with her little farm."

"The Hameau de la Reine," he said, blue eyes creasing as he smiled. "The thought crossed my mind, too, but it's not quite so extravagant. We left out the farm, the mill, the Temple of Love, the belvedere, and the grotto."

"Tell me you didn't import all those stones for the house."

"No. Thankfully the island has an abundance of stone, and we were able to use all local stone, cutting them here, which made it far easier physically, as well as more affordable."

"And yet this is still extremely costly."

"Can I not give my bride a wedding gift?"

"Will your people want my head?"

"My people are your people, and they will want you and our children happy." He drew her into his arms, kissing her, oh, so slowly and tenderly, and when he raised his head, his blue eyes were bright and warm and filled with conviction and love. "You will have more children, *cara*. It will all work out. It might just take time—"

"I know," she interrupted, standing on tiptoe to kiss him back. "And it will work out, always, as long as you and I are together and we stick together. Friends, lovers, partners." She felt the secret rise in her, the joy overwhelming. "Parents."

"Yes, we will be parents," he agreed firmly, sounding like the man who'd served his country in the Royal Navy.

"In just six months," she said, kissing him again. "And next week, we can find out the sex, if you want. Or we can both go and just look at the ultrasound and watch the baby's lovely little heart."

Alexander's jaw worked and he blinked hard, clearing the sheen gathering there. "A baby."

"Our baby."

"You've seen the doctor?"

She nodded. "I have, and I've seen the ultrasound and everything looks good. There should be no problems. I just can't go racing up and down steep stairs."

He glanced toward the water. "Or riding in bumpy speedboats. Why didn't you tell me?"

"The boat ride was fine. Trust me. And I was going to tell you this weekend. I had a special reveal planned, but this was actually so much better."

"I'm calling for the helicopter to take us home."

"Alexander."

"I'm taking no chances."

"Alexander!" she protested, laughing.

"I'm taking no chances at all. I love you, Josephine. I love you more than you'll ever know."

* * * * *

If you enjoyed
The Prince's Scandalous Wedding Vow
you're sure to enjoy these other stories
by Jane Porter!

Bought to Carry His Heir
Her Sinful Secret
His Merciless Marriage Bargain
Kidnapped for His Royal Duty

Available now!